Highland Intrigue A Prequel

by

Donna Fletcher

Donna Fletcher

No part of this publication may be used or reproduced in any manner whatsoever, including but not limited to being stored in a retrieval system or transmitted in any form or by any means, electronic, mechanical, photocopying, recording or otherwise without permission of the author.

This is a book of fiction. Names, characters, places, and incidents are either the product of the author's imagination or are used fictitiously, and any resemblance to actual persons, living or dead, business establishments, events or locales is entirely coincidental.

Highlander Intrigue A Prequel

All rights reserved.

Copyright March 2021 by Donna Fletcher

Cover art
Kim Killion Group

Visit Donna's Web site
www.donnafletcher.com

Chapter One

13th century Scotland

"Please, my lady, do not do this, come with me," Gunna begged, tears running down her full cheeks.

Tears and determination filled Lady Aila's eyes and she squeezed the woman's slim arm. "You have been more than a loyal servant to me, Gunna, you have been a kind and loyal friend. I need that friendship and loyalty now more than ever."

"I won't fail you, my lady. You have my word," Gunna said, resolve and strength forming with the tilt of her chin.

Lady Aila smiled softly. "I know you won't. That is why I tasked you with this dangerous mission. I have faith in you, Gunna, and never forget how grateful I am to you for what you do for me."

Gunna's tears continued to fall. "I wish—"

"I know. I wish the same." Lady Aila wiped at the few tears that had escaped her eyes. "Unfortunately, fate has other plans, but I won't let fate decide my daughter's destiny. She will live to decide her own. Now go and do what you must." She hugged the woman tight and turned away from her.

Lady Aila fought her tears as she hurried through the castle and when she entered the Great Hall, she gasped. Warriors were placing her husband on one of the tables. She hurried to him.

Her legs almost failed her when she caught sight of his chest covered with blood. She took his limp hand when she reached his side and she was grateful to feel his fingers close around hers though not with the strength of the mighty warrior he had always been. "Brochan."

His eyes fluttered open and he struggled to speak. "Tell me it is done."

"It is done, my love," she said, resting her cheek next to his.

Tears filled his eyes, something Aila had never seen in the eight years they had been married.

"I have always loved you, Aila, and I will miss you." He struggled to turn his head to kiss her cheek.

Aila moved her head meeting his lips in a kiss that was bittersweet. "Not for long. I will not be far behind you." She pressed her fingers to his mouth, seeing him ready to argue. "It must be done. It's the only way."

"If she is half as willful and strong as you, she will survive."

"And as brave and fearless as you. I love you, Brochan, always."

He fought with what little strength he had left to raise his hand and she helped him, resting his hand against her cheek and placing her hand over it. She held it there tight against her, not caring that it was marred with dirt and blood. She wanted to feel his touch one last time.

His hand went limp against her cheek and she watched as life faded from his eyes, and she wept.

"They're almost here, my lady, you must leave," a warrior urged.

She nodded, kissed her husband one last time, and hurried out of the room. She rushed to her bedchamber and grabbed her cloak, then went to the cradle beside the bed and picked up the small, wrapped bundle. Her tears continued to stream down her face as she hurried through the keep.

Two days. It had been barely two days since she had given birth to their daughter and two days since the Scottish crown ordered the execution of her husband and daughter so that the Clan MacWilliam would be no more. Her husband had bravely fought but it had been a losing battle and they both knew from the start that it would be. Their only hope had been to save their precious newborn bairn from losing her life before she even had a chance to start it.

Aila hugged the small bundle to her chest and took quick steps through the keep. Many of the servants had deserted them and the few warriors that remained faithful were fast falling to the enemy's sword. She had little time.

She made her way out the back of the keep and around the side. Her boots sunk into the snow on the ground, covering a good portion of them. A sharp chill stung her cheeks, and the gloom of the gray sky that hovered heavily over the village added to her despair. Her only way to the woods was through part of the village. She watched as she waited as the last of the MacWilliam warriors fell bravely one after another and when she thought the way clear, she ran.

A shout echoed through the village. "THERE SHE

IS!"

Another shout followed. "SHE HAS THE BAIRN!"

Her heart beat pounded against her chest and she prayed for strength to do what needed to be done. She ran, reaching the edge of the woods, darting around the large pines and barren oaks. The hood of her dark cloak slipped off her head, her long dark hair spilling free. She hugged the bundle tightly to her chest.

"GET THE BAIRN. KILL HER!" a warrior cried out.

Warriors suddenly surrounded her. She was trapped, there was no way out.

"It won't be long now, Brochan," she whispered.

I'm here with you, Aila. You're not alone.

The whisper of his voice in her head gave her strength and she raised her chin proudly, standing perfectly still.

The pounding of horses' hooves was heard and the circle of men parted. Three warriors, lords in their own right, brought their horses to a stop not far from her.

"Give her over and we'll let you live," the one in the middle commanded.

She looked to each of them, all three having once claimed to be her husband's friend. But her husband's opposition to what the authority of Scottish kings would mean for the Highlands were at odds and so friends became foes.

"Don't give your life needlessly, Aila," the one warrior said.

Her heart broke at Lochlann's words. He had been a good friend to her husband and to her.

"Hand over your daughter," Lochlann ordered.

When Aila didn't obey, a nod from Lochlann had a warrior step forward to rip the bundle from Aila's arms.

The warrior shook his head as he tore the bundle apart, nothing but small blankets dropping to the ground.

"Tell us where she is," Lochlann commanded.

"Never," Aila said.

"Save yourself from torture, Aila, and tell us where she is," Lochlann urged.

"No torture could be worse than the pain I suffer over the loss of my husband and that I will never see my daughter grow into a fine, brave woman. You will never find her. The MacWilliam bloodline will live on." Aila smiled and before a warrior could reach her, she grabbed the knife she had tucked in the belt at her waist and plunged it into her stomach.

Lochlann rushed off his horse and went to her, going down beside her where she lay slumped on the ground. He slipped his arm under her shoulders and lifted her some.

Blood began to dribble from Aila's mouth. "She's safe. You'll never find her. And a curse on the three of you for betraying your friend. May you suffer and never know peace until you right this terrible wrong." She struggled to continue talking. "But you, Lochlann, will suffer the worst for you were his best friend."

Aila smiled as a bolt of lightning suddenly illuminated the sky and a crack of thunder followed, sounding like an angry roar from the heavens.

Her last words were carried on the thunder as it rumbled away along with her life. "The heavens accept the curse and will see it done."

Chapter Two

About twenty years later

Bliss kept her arms around her two sisters as the two men entered the Clan Loudon village. There had been talk for weeks of these men and what their arrival meant. They were there to find a wife for the cursed lord. News had spread rapidly through the clan, alerting all to Lord MacClaren's intentions. With no noble lord allowing his daughter anywhere near the cursed lord, Lord MacClaren had resorted to looking among the peasants. He had but one son left, his other two sons having met early deaths; one in battle and the other to an illness.

There was a good reason that no noble or sane woman wanted to wed Rannick MacClaren. His family had been cursed and he had been touched by it, losing three wives in the last six years. One had died in childbirth along with the bairn, one had perished in an accident, and one had collapsed in his arms and died as if the curse had simply struck her down.

Desperate for his son to wed, Lochlann MacClaren had sent two warriors to scour the surrounding land and find his son a wife.

"They won't choose us, will they, Bliss?" Elysia

asked, her voice as gentle as her soft nature.

"I'll not let them take you, Elysia," Annis said, her hand on the hilt of her knife tucked in the sheath on her belt at her waist and a glint in her eyes that would warn away any sensible person. "I'll see them gutted before I let them take me." She turned brilliant green eyes on Bliss. "It's a good thing you're two ten and two years, well past marriage age and you don't possess round, child-bearing hips, being so rail thin."

"Annis, you're being cruel," Elysia scolded.

"Annis is only speaking the truth," Bliss said, worried over Annis, not only that she failed to measure her words, but also because she was the most beautiful lass in the village. Her long, flaming red hair highlighted her pale complexion and danced in ringlets around her lovely face. Her green eyes were as bold in color as her tongue was with her words. And her shapely body caught the eye of every man in the village, wed or not. Fortunately, her sharp tongue kept them at bay. Annis was not one for womanly chores, but would rather be engaged with the planting of the fields or the building of the shelters or sheds.

"You think me cruel and I think us lucky, for I do not want to lose Bliss," Annis said and quickly turned her head away.

As strong and determined as Annis was, she had a generous and loving heart and tears often were her enemy, sneaking up on her unexpectedly, and no matter how hard she tried to fight them, they would often fall, annoying her.

"You are right." Elysia sighed and looked to Bliss. "I do not know what we'd do without you."

"And you do not have to," Bliss assured her. "Annis is right. No one will look my way so there is no worry for me."

She wasn't sure if she needed to worry about Elysia. She was not as beautiful as Annis, but she was pretty with soft green eyes and thick, long, light brown hair that fell to the middle of her back. She often wore it piled on the top of her head with two combs that couldn't contain it all, leaving several strands to fall around her face and down her neck. Her narrow hips and small breasts would be a worrisome sign to some wise women who deliver bairns, thinking her woman passageway far too narrow for the bairn to slip through and her breasts too small to provide sufficient milk. But she never found that a problem with all the bairns she'd delivered. She did not, however, want to think about how uncomfortable it might be for Elysia when it came to coupling if she should meet a large man. Elysia also preferred the quiet. She avoided loud, boisterous people and large congregations. She enjoyed stitching and could get lost in it for hours. Many came to her with garments they thought beyond repair and when she got done, no one could tell it had been mended.

She could not rule out that the two men might take interest in Elysia, but she was more worried about Annis. She had no worries for herself, since Annis had been right. No one would look her way. Her features were nothing to speak of and she was fine with that. She probably would never wed and have bairns of her own, though she would love to. Sometimes the thought upset her since she enjoyed raising Annis and Elysia after their mum had died ten years ago. She had barely turned twelve, but she had been all her sisters had, their da having died a year before their mum. Elysia had been seven years and Annis nine years. She had quickly taken on the role of their mum and raised them with love and care just as their mum would have done.

One day they would wed good men, she would see to it, and she would help them raise their bairns.

"Do not look at the men," Bliss warned.

Elysia already had her eyes cast down, but Annis stuck her chin up defiantly and glared at the two men. It worried Bliss when the gray-haired man held her gaze far too long.

When the men rode past, Bliss turned to Annis. "And what if your defiance gets you a marriage to the cursed lord?"

"I will not marry him," Annis declared with confidence.

"And how will you stop it?" Bliss asked, putting nothing past Annis.

"I will marry someone else first."

Bliss shook her head. "And who would that be?"

"I don't know, but I better start looking just in case," Annis said and set off determined.

That gave Bliss thought. Perhaps it would be wise to find her two sisters husbands, men that would keep them safe, and men from the clan so that her sisters would not be taken away from her.

***

"How did your hunt for a husband go, Annis," Elysia asked, nibbling on the last of her bread.

It was a wasted effort," Annis complained, sopping up the last of the delicious fish stew with a chunk of bread Bliss had prepared for supper. "There's not a man among the clan who would make a good husband."

"You mean a husband who will follow your dictate." Elysia chuckled.

"What's wrong with that?" Annis snapped. "I am more intelligent than most men, so why shouldn't I command instead?"

Elysia sighed. "It is not the way of things."

Annis went to argue and Bliss stopped her. "Elysia speaks the truth as you did today about me. You cannot get angry at the truth whether you agree with it or not. It seems to be a woman's lot in life to obey her husband unless you can find a man who thinks otherwise and that, I am afraid, is unlikely."

"Then I will not wed," Annis said.

Bliss gripped her hands gently and rested them on the table in front of her. "I have been giving thought to marriage."

"*You* have been giving thought to marriage?" Annis looked aghast and shook her head. "You cannot wed. What will happen to Elysia and me?"

Bliss hurried to reassure them, seeing that Elysia had paled considerably. "Not me marrying, you two finding husbands." Her hand shot up when they both looked to protest. "Let me finish before you argue with me. And let me say that you both know I would never force you into any marriage."

Both women nodded, worry draining from their faces.

"Everyone worries that a woman will be chosen

from the clan to wed Lord Rannick of the Clan MacClaren and I certainly do not want it to be either of you. One way to ensure that and to make certain you find husbands that will suit you is to search for a husband for yourselves." Bliss stopped Annis from speaking once again. "I know you looked today, but a couple of hours today will not find you a husband. Besides, it is important to know what you each want and do not want in a husband before you even start your search."

"Like Annis not wanting a husband who will dictate to her," Elysia said.

"Or a husband that is loud and boisterous for Elysia," Annis countered.

"So true," Elysia agreed.

"And you were right for me as well," Annis said.

"I am sure you both also thought of having bairns of your own." Bliss laughed. "That is not possible without a husband."

Annis wrinkled her nose. "I do not know if I would like what needs doing for a man's seed to grow inside me, but I have thought about bairns of my own. I would love to teach my daughter things that most mums would not think to teach a lass. And I would raise my son not to dictate to his wife."

"I would love to have bairns of my own, but I fear having them. I know what the women say about me. I am too petite to accept a man between my legs." Elysia blushed. "And perhaps they're right, but I worry more when I hear them say I would not survive childbirth."

"You have delivered plenty of bairns safely," Annis said with a look to Bliss to ease Elysia's worry.

If there was one thing Bliss never did, it was lie to her sisters. They had the right to the truth and she spoke it now. "I have never found small women to have any more of a problem with their deliveries than larger ones. Small or large, one never knows what to expect when a bairn is ready to be born. And I will be there with you to make sure you do well."

"So will I," Annis said.

Elysia chuckled. "You fainted the one and only time you insisted on helping Bliss deliver a bairn. Or do you forget you faint at the sight of blood."

"I only faint when there is a lot of blood," Annis corrected. "I won't with you. I will not let myself faint. I will stay with you all the way through the delivery."

"That is thoughtful, Annis, but what about when you deliver a bairn of your own?" Elysia asked.

"That is different. I don't have to see what's happening down in the nether region. I only have to deal with the pain and that I will conquer," Annis said confidently.

Bliss could not help but smile. Annis believed she could conquer anything if she put her mind to it and Bliss wondered if one day she might discover something that was unconquerable.

"Now that we have that settled, what do you think about finding husbands for yourselves?" Bliss asked.

"I think it is a wise idea," Elysia said, a slight frown replacing her smile. "The clan women have warned me that I do not grow any younger and I should wed soon and that younger women than myself are already wed and have bairns."

"Who? Who said that? I will go tell them to—"

Elysia quickly interrupted, "I thanked them for their advice."

"You are far too sweet," Annis warned, shaking her head. She stopped suddenly and her eyes popped wide. "What did they say about me since I am two years older than you."

Elysia remained silent, her lips tightly locked.

"You better tell me," Annis threatened.

Elysia easily surrendered, knowing her sister was owed the truth. "They say you will never wed, that no man wants you."

Elysia drew back in her chair, thinking fire might spew from Annis' eyes at any moment.

"I will show those gossiping hags. I will find a husband, and a good one at that," Annis said with a firm nod that confirmed it.

"I am glad you both agree. I want to see you both happy," Bliss said.

"But what of you, Bliss?" Elysia asked. "Do you not wish to wed and have bairns of your own?"

"Let's not discuss that now. It is important you two wed and start your lives with your own families. As long as you stay close by, where we can see each other daily, then nothing else matters."

Annis pounded her fist on the table. "That is at the top of my list for a husband. He must be part of this clan so that we three stay together."

Elysia hurried to agree. "Aye, we stay together."

"Good," Bliss said relieved, fearful of losing her sisters. "Now, is there any man in the clan that either of you might favor?"

"What if the two men who arrived today chooses

one of us before we can find a husband?" Elysia asked.

"We have time," Bliss assured her. "You both know, Lendra, a friend and servant in the keep. She made sure to spread the word of what she heard. They are here to see if anyone might suit their need and to report back to Lord MacClaren. The two are going to some other clans as well, so there is time for us to see this done."

"I heard tell that two other clans were also affected by this curse that has cost the lives of two of Lord MacClaren's three sons," Annis said.

"What is this curse that has brought such heartache to the Clan MacClaren?" Elysia asked.

Annis shook her head. "I do not know and, if anyone does know, they dare not utter a word of it for fear it will somehow strike them."

"And it is better we do not speak of it so it does not strike us," Bliss warned.

Annis and Elysia nodded.

"Instead of telling me if there is anyone you favor in the clan, tell me what you each want in a husband," Bliss said.

Elysia and Annis talked over each other with their list until Bliss halted them both with a loud "STOP!"

Annis and Elysia laughed.

"You go first, Annis," Elysia offered and Annis was only too happy to oblige.

"I want a strong man but not a stubborn one. He also has to be clean. I cannot abide the stink of some of the men in the clan."

"I agree wholeheartedly," Elysia said.

"I thought you were mean when you made me

wash more than the other children, but I am so grateful you did," Annis said, then laughed. "We are so clean that it makes even a slight stink unbearable. So definitely no stinky husband. I also do not want a man who expects me to obey his every word or submit to his every whim." She lowered her voice as if afraid someone might hear her. "I heard some women talk about how demanding their husbands are in bed." She scrunched her nose. "I could not put up with that."

Bliss raised her hand and pointed to each finger as she listed what Annis wanted in a husband. "Strong husband. Not stubborn. Not stinky. Not one who expects you to obey his every word or whim. And not one who demands when it comes to coupling. Is that all?"

"No drinking himself senseless."

"Aye, definitely not that," Elysia agreed.

"And at least some intelligence," Annis added. "So we may discuss interesting things."

Bliss nodded. "No heavy drinker and some intelligence. Now you must keep all those things in mind when you look for a husband, and I will do the same as I search for one that might suit you." She turned to Elysia. "Your turn."

"I do not want a man so large that he looks as if he will consume me," she said with a shiver. "I prefer him to be slim and not too tall since I am short. He does not need to talk much, since I prefer things quiet. I would like him to be thoughtful and gentle." She shook her head. "No warrior. No man so skillful with a sword he is feared." She shivered again. "I would not mind if he worked one of the crofts, where it would be quiet, though it would have to be a short distance from the village." She smiled at Bliss. "So I could come and spend time with you every day."

Bliss returned the smile and held up her hand to once again point at her fingers as she listed what type of husband Elysia wanted. "No large man. Slim and not too tall. Doesn't talk much. Likes the quiet. Thoughtful and gentle. Definitely no warrior. Not overly skillful with a sword. Can live in one of the crofts but a short walk to the keep."

"How about that man who moved into one of the crofts about a month ago? He stays to himself and doesn't say much when he comes to market day," Annis said. "I think someone mentioned he was a friend of Chieftain Emory. I believe his name is Saber."

Elysia shook her head. "I saw him briefly. He is far too large and too thick with muscles. He would easily squash me with one hug."

"Maybe he's thoughtful and gentle," Annis said with a teasing smile.

Elysia did not find her sister amusing, shaking her head as she cast her eyes down at the table top. "How can a man that large be gentle? No, I have no interest in him."

"How about Moray?" Bliss suggested, seeing how upset the thought of the large man affected her sister and sent Annis a scolding look.

Annis at least looked contrite and attempted to help ease her sister's upset. "Moray might not be bad for you, Elysia. He is not too tall and he's thin and he speaks softly. He does not have bad features, though his nose is a bit crooked from Clyde punching him that one time. He has little skill with a sword preferring bow and arrow, and he should since it's his craft."

"I suppose he does have possibilities," Elysia agreed.

"But you hesitate," Bliss said. "Why?"

"I do not know." Elysia shrugged. "He seems nice when he speaks with me."

"Why don't you make an effort to speak with him and see what you think," Bliss suggested. "In the meantime, we will think of others that might suit you, and as well for you, Annis."

Annis yawned loudly. "I can wait until tomorrow. I am up with first light. Duff is actually taking some of my suggestions when it comes to the new shed and he wants me there when they start building it. Now if only he wasn't so old. I would marry him in a minute. He is a fine looking man and we enjoy talking about how buildings go together, and he does not stink."

"That is because his wife takes good care of him and he is good to her," Bliss said.

"There is one thing that would not have worked between you two," Elysia said with a twinkle in her eyes.

Curiosity had Annis asking, "What is that?"

"He and his wife have six children, which means he likes to couple." Elysia chuckled.

Annis wrinkled her nose and shook her head. "Now I am going to have a difficult time looking at him tomorrow. I am off to bed and hopefully forget that you said that."

Bliss went to bed after her sisters, a habit of hers, always making sure they were tucked in safely. She laid awake unable to sleep, her mind churning. It might not be too difficult to find a husband for Elysia, but she feared it might be impossible to find a husband for Annis. She had a lot of work to do to see them both safely wed to good men. She fell asleep with prayers on her lips that she'd be able to do so.

Chapter Three

It was market day in the village. There was much Bliss needed to get, but she was concerned when she caught sight of Lord MacClaren's two men perusing the market. Mothers grabbed their daughters and turned them away from the men, the older of the two men paying no mind to their actions.

Bliss gave a quick glance around, looking for her sisters. She did not spot them and for that she was grateful. If she did not see them, then neither did the two men. She shivered at the thought that Elysia or Annis could be whisked away to meet a horrible fate as the wife of the cursed lord.

She turned her attention back to the market stalls and bumped into Lendra from the keep. The woman tugged her away from the crowd of busy people to a quiet spot.

"I have news," Lendra whispered, "and I tell you we are lucky we have plain features and few men look our way."

She and Lendra were close in age and they did have plain features, but where Lendra had a full shape, Bliss was thin with barely a shape to her. And Lendra had been kind including herself when saying few men looked their way. Bliss had seen more than a few men look Lendra's way with interest, yet never had a man shown interest in her.

"Mothers are searching for husbands for their daughters, but it will do no good," Lendra said.

Bliss's stomach churned, since she had thought the same for her sisters, and she feared what Lendra would say.

"The two men not only search for a wife for the cursed lord but for the other two lords' sons who were doomed by the curse as well. That is three women they search for and Chieftain Emory has been ordered to ban all marriages until further notice. He will make the announcement today."

Bliss felt herself pale. Now what was she to do?

"You better watch out for Annis. She is far too beautiful to go unnoticed," Lendra warned. "I must go and spread the word so that mothers and daughters are not caught unaware."

"I appreciate you telling me, Lendra," Bliss said and the woman took off.

Bliss took a few moments to calm herself before going to find Elysia and Annis and tell them the news, though they might learn it before she could find them. She silently berated herself for not seeing her sisters wed sooner. But neither had voiced any interest in marrying yet, and she selfishly hadn't wanted to lose them.

She hurried through the market and seeing the worried looks on many of the mothers' faces meant the news was spreading fast. She strained her neck looking about for her sisters and spotted the two men talking to a mother and daughter, the mother keeping her arm wrapped tightly around the lass.

The older man turned as the younger man

continued to question the mother. He looked straight at Bliss and held her eyes for a moment. He turned back to the mother and after speaking to her, the woman pointed to Bliss, nodding.

The two men approached her and she thought to hurry away, but she feared they would chase after her, and then she would draw attention to Elysia and Annis. It was better she remained where she was and see what they wanted.

"You are the clan healer?" the older man asked.

Bliss had trouble thinking of herself as the clan healer. However, before Kendesa, the old healer, had died months ago, she claimed Bliss the new healer. She did not feel she knew half as much as Kendesa had, but people came to her anyway and she treated them the best she could. So she had no choice but to nod, confirming it so.

"We have a man arriving here tomorrow who needs care. You will tend him," the younger man ordered.

She nodded again and the young man walked away, his eyes searching the crowd. The older man stared at her a moment before smiling pleasantly and with a nod he walked off. Her heart was thumping so fast that she placed her hand to her chest and took slow breaths to calm it.

Whatever was she going to do? How was she going to protect her sisters?

Her heart beat faster and she hurried off, needing to find her sisters and rush them home.

***

Elysia spotted the two men who searched for a wife for the dreadful cursed lord and shivered. They were not far off and she hurried to turn and keep a safe distance from them. She bumped into something hard and stumbled back, disoriented. Suddenly, a hand closed around her arm so tight she thought a shackle had clamped around it. She raised her eyes slowly along the length of the man. He was broad in width, his chest wide and muscled, and he devoured her short height. His dark wool cloak lay open and the garments beneath were just as dark as the cloak. His neck was swathed in cloth and she wasn't sure if she wanted to look upon his face. The only way to do it was to be quick about it. She tilted her head back and almost gasped when she was met with intense green eyes. They frightened and yet captivated, especially since the swath of cloth around his neck extended up and across the lower portion of his face, leaving only his eyes to look upon.

"I—I—I am sorry," Elysia sputtered and yanked her arm free surprised it released so easily. She turned to run and spotted the two men growing closer. Instinct had her turning and hurrying behind the large man to hide. "Please do not move," she begged in a whisper. "I do not want those two men to see me."

She remained huddled as close to his back as she could, though he was so wide and tall, she doubted anyone could spot her cowering behind him. He had a strong scent about him, pine, fresh earth, and a slight odor of wood smoke, a favorable combination.

Elysia was startled when he turned slowly, allowing her time to turn with him so she would not be spotted until she wound up as if engulfed in his arms. His scent grew stronger around her and she found herself stepping closer to him until their bodies brushed against each other.

A chilled early autumn air had lingered since dawn and though she had worn her wool cloak and was warm enough, the warmth of the man's large body provided a more comforting heat.

When she almost laid her head on his chest, she realized his nearness had intoxicated her and she quickly raised her head. Her words stumbled out once again. "I—I—I am sorry for imposing on you."

She peeked past his broad shoulders and was relieved to see the two men gone and Bliss heading her way. She looked up at him again. "My sister is here. Thank you for shielding me."

He gave a nod, turned, and walked away.

"Thank God I found you," Bliss said. "We have to find Annis and go home. I have news and it is not good."

***

Annis had found Bliss and Elysia, having heard the news and was anxious to see if either had heard yet.

"I cannot believe Chieftain Emory is going to ban marriages until further notice," Annis said, pacing in front of the closed door once the three had settled inside the cottage. "What of the marriages that were to take place?" She stopped. "Chieftain Emory would not let those women be taken away, would he?"

"That would be terrible," Elysia said and looked to

Bliss.

"I do not know what Chieftain Emory would do," Bliss said, fearing the powerful dictates of nobles." She turned a stern eye on Annis. "What I do know is that you need to keep as far away from those two men as possible. Give them no reason to take notice of you."

Annis nodded and wrapped her arms tight around herself. "I heard some things about the cursed lord, but I am not sure if I should believe what I have heard."

Elysia leaned forward at the table, keeping her voice low as if afraid someone would hear them. "What did you hear?'

Annis leaned forward as well. "I heard two men talking. They said that the cursed lord has gone insane. That after he killed his wives, he sailed off to foreign soil where his skin has shaded from the bright sun and where he got two scars on his face from the many battles he fought. They said his father sent men to get him and the men returned battered and bruised, some with broken bones, it not having been an easy task to return his son home. They said he is more a wild animal than he is human."

Elysia shivered and Bliss's stomach churned.

"They also talked about the other two men the curse touched. They say the one lost his voice the day his brother died while others say he killed his brother in a fit of madness. The other cursed man suffers differently. He is so cursed that death will not even touch him. He has been condemned to walk the earth and never die. He has suffered wounds that should have taken his life. He was even hung once but it did not kill him and he was caught in a rushing stream that spit him out soon after he entered it."

Elysia turned fearful eyes on Bliss. "What are we to do?"

Bliss did not care for her own answer. "I do not know. There is no place for us to go, to hide. We can only pray the two men will not find favor with either of you."

"I am frightened, Bliss," Elysia said, pulling the shawl she wore tighter around her.

"I would admit this to no one but the two of you," Annis said with a nod to each. "I am frightened as well."

"I feel the same," Bliss said, hating to admit it. "I have kept you both safe all these years, but I fear there is nothing I can do if one of you is chosen and the thought frightens me down to my soul. The only thing left to us is to stay strong and pray."

Bliss laid awake on her makeshift pallet on the floor while her sisters slept soundly, tucked in the only bed in the one room cottage. There had to be something she could do. Something that would help keep her sisters safe. She recalled what the old healer had told her before she died. If ever a problem presented itself that was too difficult or seemed impossible to handle, she should go seek the help of the wise woman in the woods… Cumina.

Many were frightened of her, believing her a witch, though they sought her help when needed. She was known for her amulets and potions, but she refused to cast a curse. That meant she had knowledge of curses. And with that knowledge, she would know how a curse could be broken.

***

Morning dawned busy and with having to remain available to tend whoever it was the two men had told her would arrive today in need of care, Bliss had no hope of going to see Cumina today.

"I wish Annis would not have taken the chance and gone out this morning," Elysia said, voicing her worry that was even more obvious in the cloth that lay in her lap and had gone untouched by the bone needle clasped between her fingers. Her fingers never stilled when she held a needle. They flew across cloth like magic.

"Annis's endless curiosity would never allow her to remain confined to the cottage for long. Besides, the two men will not look in the fields or bother with the men busy building, leaving Annis safe for the moment." Bliss hoped such reassurance would calm Elysia's worry.

It struck some hope in Elysia as did her own thought. "Perhaps her lack and disinterest in wifely duties will save her."

"A good thought and one I hope proves true," Bliss said.

The door burst open, startling the two.

"Do you know who approaches?" Annis asked, her cheeks red and her breath labored from running, though the latter didn't stop her from answering her own question. "The condemned lord. The one who cannot die, who is forever doomed to walk this earth."

"No one escapes death," Bliss said.

"A curse could make it so," Annis argued.

"Everyone is gathering to see him."

"Good Lord," Elysia said, dropping the needle in her lap. "He is the one they need you to tend, Bliss."

Annis paled and her loss of words showed just how worried she was for Bliss.

"I am in no danger. I will tend him and all will be fine," Bliss assured them both.

"With his numerous close calls of death, what if it is decided it was best for him to wed a healer?" Elysia suggested.

Annis was quick to tell more. "I heard say that he favors any type woman, small, tall, wide, skinny, pretty or ugly. It doesn't matter to him. He eagerly pokes any woman."

"Annis!" Elysia scolded. "You do not think before you speak. You insult our sister with your suggestion that her looks make no difference."

"I do no such thing, though it would be a good thing if he does not choose her," Annis argued. "I only tell you what I hear and I bet no one wants to poke him since they fear him a doomed man."

"Bliss!" a shout came from outside.

Bliss recognized Lendra's voice and opened the door.

"Chieftain Emory sent me for you. He wants you at the keep to tend the man entering the village now." She lowered her voice to a whisper. "He is one of the three men who are doomed by the curse. He is the condemned one." She grabbed Bliss's arm, fright having turned her eyes wide. "He says to bring one of your sisters in case you require an extra hand."

Elysia gasped.

"We will be right there," Bliss said, her stomach roiling so badly she feared she would lose her breakfast.

"Bless you both," Lendra said with teary eyes and hurried away.

"I will go," Annis said, leaning down to make certain her knife was tucked safely in her boot.

Bliss preferred neither of her sisters accompanied her, but she had little choice in the matter. But how did she decide which one?

"I should go. We need to keep Annis away from those two men," Elysia said. "Besides, she is not good at the sight of a lot of blood."

"I can manage," Annis argued.

"So you will be all right if he is oozing or flowing with blood and some of it touches your hands or gets on your garments? And you will have no trouble wiping away caked blood if necessary?" Elysia continued.

Annis turned away gagging and when she turned back her face was sickly pale. "It is better that you go, seeing how good you are with a needle you could stitch wounds as beautifully as you stitch cloth."

Bliss had felt the pain of loss when their da had died and then their mum, but never had she reason to feel the pain of defeat and that was what she felt now listening to her sisters. They needed to hear the truth of their situation, whether any of them wanted to face it or not.

"We must face the truth," Bliss said with a heavy heart. "We are foolish to think we can avoid those men. They will seek out every woman in the village without exception and choose without care."

"I do not like my fate left to another," Annis said.

Elysia offered her own worry. "I do not like feeling so vulnerable."

"And I cannot bear the thought that I cannot protect either of you from this," Bliss said. "But right now, we are together and God willing we will stay that way."

It was decided after some debate that Annis would go and she and Bliss headed to the keep. Elysia remained in the cottage, having no desire to leave the quiet and safety it provided her. She got busy stitching, knowing the chore would chase her worries away at least for a while.

The knock at the door startled her and while she would have preferred not to answer it, it could be someone in need of healing. If it was a minor problem she could tend it, since she had learned quite a bit helping her sister, anything more and they would have to wait until Bliss returned.

Elysia drew back when she opened the door, the man who she had hid behind on market day consuming the doorway with his large frame. His eyes were still the only part of his face she could see, the lower portion remaining covered. The intensity of his bold green eyes put a fright in her as did his size. It overwhelmed.

He looked to his hand that he held out to her and pointed to his middle finger.

"Oh my," Elysia said and stepped forward to gently place her hand beneath his, though his spilled over her small one, completely covering it. "That is terribly red and swollen. It must hurt." She raised her head to see him nod. "Bliss is not here, but I may be able to help you if you would like me to."

He nodded again.

"Sit at the table while I gather some things," she said with a pleasant smile and she was glad she had a reason to leave the cottage for a moment and escape his intense eyes that intimidated far too easily. She stepped outside and took a deep breath, though the image of his green eyes she feared were forever branded in her mind. She shook her head at the foolish thought and filled a bucket from the rain barrel and entered the cottage.

She placed the bucket on the table in front of him and almost gasped. The swath of cloth that had covered part of his face lay at his neck and Elysia was shocked by his exceptional features. They were as handsome and intense as his green eyes and just as intimidating.

"You need to soak your finger in the water," she instructed, after scooping up some water in a wooden bowl and placing it in front of him. Then she hurried to turn away without seeing if he did what she asked, but she caught his movement out of the corner of her eye and assumed he did.

She gathered what she needed and placed them on the table, then placed two candles she lit from the hearth's flames and placed them on the table to have better light.

Elysia gasped when she looked at him, her hand going to her own neck after seeing the angry scar that ran along his neck. "Is that scar how you lost your voice?" she asked softly.

He did not acknowledge her. He did not have to, his eyes were answer enough and their forceful scrutiny warned her not to pursue it. She turned away and silently cautioned herself to hold her tongue. What happened to him was no concern of hers, but she couldn't help but feel sorry for him.

She took his hand out of the water and patted it dry. She held it near the candle's flame so she could see the wound better and smiled. "Just as I thought, a splinter. I can mend this for you."

He nodded.

She retrieved her bone needle and held it in front of him. "This may hurt a bit."

He nodded again, accepting his fate.

She tried to find the right position to work on his finger, the closer the better, but she found none that would work the best. Until she was suddenly settled on his leg, his arm around her waist and her legs left to dangle just above the floor. She looked up at him and he raised his brow as if challenging her to object.

"I suppose this is the best position," she said, his action not at all proper, but feeling it better that she did not object.

He nodded and she went to work, trying to ignore his size and recalled how she had felt lost in his embrace when he had hidden her from those two men. But she had also felt safe as she did now, a surprising thought.

She brought the needle to his finger and focused on nothing else but retrieving the splinter. He did not move once, though she knew it had to have hurt, the splinter deep. She cleaned the wound with a wet cloth when done, dried it, then smeared honey over it before tying a cloth around it.

She realized she hadn't needed to remain sitting on his leg to finish the task. But then he hadn't let go of her waist, which had her moving to slip off his leg. His arm locked on her waist as if he didn't intend to let her go, then after a few moments he eased her off his leg.

He was strong yet gentle and the thought sent a flutter through her stomach.

She turned a smile on him. "It should stay covered for a few days. If the cloth comes off, come back and I will apply a fresh one and also more honey if needed."

He nodded and stood, and she had to crane her neck back to look up at him since he stood so close. His familiar, pleasant woodsy scent drifted around her and he stared at her a moment. She wondered what he thought, what he would say if he could speak. Then he went to the door, opened it, turned back and sent her a firm nod, and was gone.

Elysia sat, feeling a bit overwhelmed by it all and realized she was smiling. He might be a big man but he was a quiet and calming man and she liked that about him. She wished she knew his name—it struck her then, what Annis had said about the large man occupying one of the crofts.

Saber.

Annis had said his name was Saber. She smiled knowing his name and got the feeling he'd be back.

She laughed lightly at herself. "Or is it that you want him to return, Elysia?"

Chapter Four

"You will stay close by my side. You will not wander away or go off with anyone. You will say I need you, that you must stay with me," Bliss ordered.

"You do not trust anyone, do you?" Annis whispered as her sister had done as she looked around the large Great Hall where a servant had deposited them when they had arrived a few moments ago.

"I do not trust the men who search for a bride. They will cart a woman off without a thought, as if she was nothing more than chattel," Bliss warned.

"I have the same instincts," Annis said, agreeing with her sister.

Bliss tugged at Annis's hand to be quiet when she spotted the older of the two men enter the room and approach them.

"I am Lawler," the gray-haired man said when he stopped in front of the two women.

Bliss acknowledged him with a nod but didn't introduce her sister. He would have to ask if he wished to know, but she had a feeling the man already knew who Annis was. The man might be aged, but his blue eyes were as vibrant and attentive as a young man's.

"You will tell me if you require anything. I must warn you that the man you will tend can be difficult, but he will not harm you."

Bliss nodded, not sure what to say, and worried

what Annis would do if the man should prove difficult.
"Come and let us get this done with," Lawler said.
Bliss kept Annis behind her. They barely had climbed the stairs when they heard the shouting.
"I DO NOT GIVE A BLOODY HELL! I DO NOT NEED A HEALER!"
The other person shouted just as loud. "IT IS NOT YOUR CHOICE!"
"IT DAMN WELL IS!" came the quick reply.
Lawler shook his head before opening the door and announcing loudly. "The healer is here!"
Bliss kept Annis tucked behind her as she followed Lawler into the room.
"Well at last I have a pretty face to look upon."
"Good, you find the healer pretty, take her for a wife. She will serve you well since you are constantly near death."
"Enough, Cadell," Lawler admonished.
It was obvious the older man was in charge since Cadell remained silent.
"I may be condemned, Cadell, but I would never condemn a woman along with me. Now get out and let the healer waste her time with me when we both know I will heal no matter what."
"As you wish, Lord Brogan," Lawler said and snapped his hand at Cadell. The man scowled and petulantly stomped out of the room. Lawler looked to Bliss. "Buckets of water sit by the hearth as well as cloths. If you need anything else, please call out. I will be waiting outside the door." With that he closed the door,
"Who hides behind you?" Brogan demanded.

Bliss's hand shot out to stop her sister from coming out from behind her, but it did not matter. The command in Brogan's voice was enough for her sister to take a stance.

"I do not hi—"

Annis lost all color when she turned her eyes on him. Brogan did not hesitate, he rushed at her as her eyes rolled back in her head and her body dropped. He scooped her up in his arms before she hit the floor. She was light, barely any weight at all, and he carried her to the large bed and placed her down on it.

Bliss stood beside him, hurrying to explain. "My sister cannot take the sight of too much blood."

"And she is a healer?" he asked, though he did not take his eyes off Annis. Her beauty captivated the senses. He had known many women but none matched her stunning beauty. He actually felt a catch to his heart as if it had stopped beating for a moment as he stared at her.

"Heavens, no," Bliss said, "but I was told to bring her along." She thought it best not to let him know she had another sister.

"Tend her, then you can see to me," Brogan ordered and turned away, feeling himself grow aroused just looking at the gorgeous woman in his bed.

"It is best I tend you first. At least by then I'll have some of the blood cleaned off you and Annis may fair better when looking upon you," Bliss said, offering a congenial smile.

"Have it your way," Brogan said and returned to the chair by the hearth.

Bliss got busy adding a mixture of leaves to one of

the buckets of water and soaking a couple of cloths in it. Even with all the blood on him, she could tell he was a man of handsome features. He wore only his plaid, the strip of cloth that usually crossed the chest hanging down from his side, leaving his chest bare. He was well built for his tall height, sheer muscle and not an ounce of fat. His fine shape could be the reason he had survived death so many times, though if the tale about him surviving a hanging was true, that was one she could not explain.

She liked to talk to the people she tended, learn about them, since it helped with their healing. She rinsed a cloth and started on his face, though she had found no wounds there. It was splattered blood that covered him.

"It must have been some fight you were in," Bliss said.

"The three bastards thought they could take me down… fools," Brogan muttered.

He had fought three men, without help, and survived. That was impressive, but she did not comment on it. She uncovered a couple of bruises as she cleaned his face, but none were extreme. The more she uncovered the more her assessments of his features proved true. He had the finest features she had ever seen on a man, including his light blue eyes. They could easily steal a woman's heart and common sense.

"Was it a quick fight?" Bliss asked, finishing up his face to move to his neck, cleaning it thoroughly.

"Quick enough after I broke the first bloke's arm."

"One had a knife, I see," she said with a nod to the wound on his left arm.

Brogan laughed, glancing down at it. "If he knew how to use it, I might have been in trouble. You will find most of the blood is not mine. I could have tended myself."

"You are right, but since I am here I may as well see to it." Bliss heard her sister stirring. "Stay there, Annis, until I tell you otherwise."

"I fainted?" Annis asked as if she didn't quite believe it.

Brogan laughed. "You did and would have hit the floor if I had not caught you."

She groaned and sat up, hurrying to look herself over. "BLOOD, BLISS! BLOOD! He got blood on me!"

Brogan laughed again. "You better go see to her."

"It will not take but a moment," Bliss said and hurried to rinse a clean cloth in the bucket before going to her sister. "It is not much at all," she assured Annis when she saw that her sister had her eyes clamped shut and her arm stuck straight out from her side.

"Look me over and see if you see any more blood," Annis begged, keeping her eyes firmly shut.

Bliss examined her thoroughly and cleaned off a few more spots. "No more blood."

"Are you sure?" Annis asked, yet to open her eyes.

"I am sure," Bliss assured her. "Now stay here until I say otherwise."

"Have no worries about that," Annis said and opened her eyes a pinch.

Bliss returned to Brogan and got busy finishing cleaning him off, knowing Annis would turn restless.

"You should thank me, Annis, for saving you from

hitting the floor," Brogan said, a teasing twinkle in his eyes.

"The floor would have been preferable." Annis shot back.

Brogan laughed. "You wound my heart, woman."

"You are lucky I do not wound something else."

"Annis!" Bliss scolded. "Remember who you talk to."

"A bloody idiot that's who," Annis called out.

Brogan chuckled, finding the beautiful woman entertaining. "There are many who would agree with you."

"Then I am among the wise ones."

"Annis!" Bliss scolded again.

"He asked for it." Annis shot back.

Brogan could not keep the chuckle out of his voice. "That is a first, I usually do not have to ask a woman."

"Not all women know better than to poke a fool."

"Enough, Annis!" Bliss reprimanded.

The door flew open.

"Why do I hear loud shouts and what is that woman doing in your bed?" Lawler demanded.

"I put her there," Brogan said. "Now leave and let the healer tend me."

Lawler went to argue.

"That is an order, Lawler," Brogan commanded with authority and the man did as he was told.

"Do not come over here, Annis," Bliss ordered, hearing her sister shifting around on the bed.

"Worry not. I have no intention of looking upon the bloody fool."

"I would reconsider, since I am the handsomest

man you will ever see," Brogan said, enjoying the teasing banter with the beautiful woman.

"I would think twice about that assumption, since it was not fine features that made me faint," Annis said loud enough for him to hear.

He could not help but continue to tease her. "I was just too *bloody* handsome for you."

Annis gagged.

His smile faltered, and he whispered to Bliss, "Is she truly gagging?"

"Unfortunately, yes," Bliss said.

"Go to her," Brogan ordered.

Bliss did so without hesitation, the strength of his command not to be ignored. She hurried the wet, clean cloth she had scooped up to the back of Annis's neck. "Slow breaths and think on Duff and what you might learn from him today."

Annis did as her sister said and waved her away, silently letting her know she was all right.

Bliss returned to Brogan, eager to be done and get Annis out of there.

"Is Duff her husband?' Brogan asked quietly.

Bliss was not one to lie, but to protect her sisters, she would. However, lying to him would do no good. If she told him Annis was married, he would find out soon enough it was untrue.

"No. Duff is a knowledgeable builder. It is why many of our structures stand firm and keep us well heated in the cold of winter. Annis is interested in such things and he kindly instructs her."

"Unusual for a woman," he said and found himself even more interested and curious about Annis.

"Unusual to meet a woman with a mind of her own?" Annis accused snappishly.

Bliss shook her head. "She also has superior hearing."

Brogan's smile returned. "Most women have a mind of their own and it is usually used to constantly nag at men."

"A wasteful effort," Annis said.

Bliss hurried to finish, seeing that Brogan was enjoying sparring with Annis far too much.

"Useless as well since men do as they please," Brogan said.

"With no thought to others," Annis argued.

"I give thought and I'm thoughtful to every woman I am with," Brogan boasted.

"Praise yourself often, do you?" Annis asked with obvious sarcasm.

Brogan laughed. "As much and as often as possible."

"And here I thought the ladies would be eager to sing your praise."

"More like shout it," Brogan boasted again with a hint of laughter.

Bliss stepped behind Brogan, hoping to catch her sister's attention so she could shake her head at her in hopes she would hold her tongue. Unfortunately, Annis kept her head turned away.

"Poor souls, you tortured them that badly?" Annis asked with a chuckle of her own.

His response ran a shiver through Bliss.

"Why don't you come here and find out for yourself, *leannan*?"

His banter had turned suggestive and that meant he was interested in Annis, and her sister did not realize it.

Annis was far too quick to respond. "I prefer not to be disappointed."

"That is something I never do, *leannan*— disappoint a woman. Spend the night with me and I will prove it." He had not planned to invite her to his bed, but there was something about her that enticed him. He did not know quite what it was, but he wanted to find out.

That had Annis jumping off the bed and racing over to him to give him a tongue lashing. As soon as her eyes landed on his freshly cleaned face, she halted abruptly. The man's handsome features stole her breath.

"I can tell that you like what you see. I can guarantee you will more than enjoy coupling with me."

His remark was like icy cold water thrown in her face and her finger jutted out to poke at his bare, hard chest. "There is nothing in this entire world that would make me couple with you, I would die first."

"Some women have told me that I bring them such exquisite pleasure they could almost die from it." He snagged her around the waist and tugged her closer to him. "I dare you to find out and deny it."

"God, you are an arrogant arse," she said and gave his chest a hard shove.

Bliss was relieved he released her sister without protest.

"If truth is arrogant, then I am guilty," he claimed, standing and holding his hands up in surrender. He realized his mistake when all color left Annis's face and once again he caught her in his arms before she hit the floor. He turned to Bliss. "I forgot the blood on my garment would be more visible to her when I stood."

Bliss pointed to the bed.

Brogan carried her over to it and reluctantly laid her down, wishing she would remain there for the night. He found he quite liked the feel of her in his arms. He had never enjoyed speaking with a woman as much as he did with Annis.

Bliss left her sister to wake from her faint and looked to Brogan. "I beg you, my lord, please do not force Annis to share your bed. It will not go well. Annis is not one to be forced. Besides, would you not prefer a willing, experienced woman."

"Are you offering yourself?"

Bliss raised her chin and her courage. "I am neither, but I would if you spared my sister."

"Annis is lucky to have such a loving, unselfish sister." He looked down at Annis, seeing that she was beginning to stir awake. "Fear not, I force no woman. She either comes to me willingly or not at all."

"I am grateful, my lord," Bliss said with a bob of her head.

"I would warn you though, Annis is a beauty. Find her a husband before a man less scrupulous than me takes an interest in her."

"Less scrupulous? I thought you were the bottom of the barrel," Annis said without opening her eyes.

"Your mouth—"

"Stings as it should to one who lacks manners," Annis scolded.

"Not what I planned to say," he said and lowered his face over hers so close their noses almost touched.

"Your mouth is delectable."

She went to retaliate and found his lips plastered to hers. His lips clung tightly and his tongue breeched the slight parting of her lips to slip into her mouth and chase her tongue. What was worse was that the pressure of his lips and his darting tongue shot a sensation through her that was actually enjoyable.

He left her mouth as quickly as he claimed it and winked at her. "See what you will miss."

Annis was glad he walked away, since her hand was itching to slap him. Not a wise thing for her to do to a nobleman.

"You both may leave. I have no more need of you, though, Annis," —he turned to face her— "you are welcome in my bed anytime."

Bliss turned a scowl on Annis and her sister wisely held her tongue. She hurried to gather her healing basket after helping her sister out of bed and sent her to wait near the door.

She handed a small crock to Brogan. "Spread this yarrow salve on your wound. It will help heal it and thank you, my lord."

He nodded and took the crock.

Bliss opened the door and could not push her sister out fast enough. That Brogan favored her was obvious and she worried that he might fail to keep his word. Or worse, Lawler might get wind of his interest and cart her sister off to wed Brogan whether he wanted to or not.

Lawler gave a nod to the two women as they hurried past him and he entered the room. He knew Brogan well, he being a good friend of Rannick's. One look at Brogan deep in thought and staring at the door told him that one of the women had caught his eye, and it was not the healer.

Chapter Five

Bliss slipped on her wool cloak. The years had worn the wool down but Elysia's talent with a needle had kept it in fair shape.

"The deep forest holds a heavy chill or you may be caught in a sudden rainfall. You should take your shawl as well," Elysia advised and handed her sister a brown shawl. She grabbed Bliss's hand when she went to take the shawl. "I know where you go."

"Say nothing to anyone, especially Annis, and see that she does not go near the keep, not that I think she will, but you never know what she will do when riled."

"You truly think Lord Brogan was attracted to her?" Elysia asked.

"I saw interest in his eyes and if I saw it, that man Lawler did as well. If he believes Lord Brogan favors Annis, then he will arrange a marriage between them even if Lord Brogan objects."

"Good Lord, Annis would never agree to the arrangement," Elysia said, upset over the possibility.

Bliss shook her head. "Which would create even more of a problem."

Elysia lowered her voice. "What makes you think the wise woman can help you?"

"It is the only thing I can think of to do. She is wise when it comes to amulets and protection. She might know what can be done to break the curse, then no wives will be needed for the three doomed men. I fear Annis being taken from us and I can think of nothing else that can prevent that, then to break the curse."

"You will be careful," Elysia said, worried for her safety.

"The old woman is harmless. I have nothing to fear from her. I only seek her advice, her wisdom in this matter. Now let me be off so I may return before dusk." Bliss hugged Elysia, trying to reassure her, though worry remained in her lovely eyes.

Bliss opened the door and took a quick step back. A man's large bulk filled the whole doorway.

He looked past Bliss to Elysia and held up his bandaged finger.

"Oh, that needs a clean wrapping. Come in and I will take care of that," Elysia offered.

Bliss turned to her sister. "Shall I stay and help?"

"No, I can see to him as I did the last time. He is the one I told you about with the splinter."

The man stepped back away from the door to give Bliss room to leave.

Bliss stopped right in front of him and felt as if the size of him swallowed her whole. "Elysia told me you were a gentleman. I expect you to remain so."

He gave a quick nod.

Bliss walked off, worried she should stay yet knowing it was imperative she go. She had to trust Elysia's opinion of the man, but Elysia could be far too trusting and kind for her own good. She struggled with her thoughts as she continued walking.

Elysia watched her sister and was glad when her pace quickened. She feared Bliss would forego her plan, not comfortable with leaving her alone with the large man. But when she quickened her pace, Elysia knew her decision to seek the old woman was more important for all of them.

She waved the man in. "Come in and let me see to that for you, Saber. Your name is Saber?"

He nodded, not seeming surprised that she knew his name and took a seat without being told and rested his hand on the table.

After Elysia gathered all she needed, Saber reached out, snagged her around the waist, and set her on his leg as he had done the last time he was here.

Elysia did not think it necessary but she also did not object. There was something comforting about being close to him, about the strength of his leg beneath her bottom, about feeling safe with him. His large size would have normally frightened her, but the short time she had spent with him allowed her to believe he had a gentle soul. She carefully unwrapped the soiled bandage and smiled. "It heals well." She turned a tender gaze on his face and the bold color of his green eyes— far bolder than her soft green eyes—sent flutters through her stomach. Or was it the way he looked at her so intensely? While the flutters remained, she cleared her head to say, "If you would not mind, I would like to see if I can help you regain your voice."

He opened his mouth to speak but nothing came out and frustration flared in his eyes.

Elysia was quick to soothe his annoyance. "After I see to your finger, I will prepare a brew for you to drink. My sister uses a particular concoction to heal problems with the throat. There is also a syrup she makes from bramble berries that is used for throat soreness. Perhaps a regiment of both will help restore your voice. That is if you are willing."

He nodded and she smiled.

She got busy cleaning the wound on his finger and coated it with honey, recalling that was what Bliss had had her do to a similar wound. She thought to use yarrow salve, but if she remembered correctly, that was used on more serious wounds.

"You will need to come here at least every other day to take the syrup and drink the brew. Can you do that?"

He tapped her arm.

Surprisingly, she understood what he asked. "Aye, I will see to administering both unless you prefer my sister to do it, which I perfectly understand, since she is the healer."

He shook his head rapidly and tapped her arm.

"You want me to take care of it for you?" she asked to make sure she understood him correctly and seeing the delight in his eyes as he nodded eagerly, she was once again struck with a rash of flutters and also a broad smile. "I would be pleased to do it for you."

A hint of a smile touched his lips as he nodded, confirming he felt the same.

The flutters continued undaunted. Never had she found a man attractive until now and never had she felt as comfortable with any man as she did with Saber, though she barely knew him. And he truly was not at all the type of man she thought she would be attracted to, being so large. However, he seemed to have a quiet manner and a gentle nature, and she favored both.

"When I am done with your wound, I will prepare the concoction for you to drink and the syrup for you to take. I will try not to keep you too long." The truth was she wanted to keep him there with her. He might not be able to speak but his presence somehow soothed her, brought a comfort of sorts that she could not explain.

He shook his head and pointed to the door.

"You are not in a rush to leave?" she asked or was that what she hoped he was trying to tell her?

He nodded, confirming that was what he meant.

She smiled again. "That is good, for it is better you drink the brew slowly and let it soothe your throat. Then I will give you the syrup before you take your leave."

She stood and cleaned the table off, then got busy setting the concoction to brew. "You work one of the crofts outside the village?"

He nodded, keeping his eyes on her, watching her every movement.

"It must be quiet there. I favor the quiet. The village is lovely but noisy with constant chatter. I escape it when I can. I take a wander in the woods or enjoy the emptiness of the cottage when my sisters are not here." She smiled. "Though I am always glad when they return."

Saber's head jerked quickly toward the door as Elysia reached down near the hearth.

A knock sounded just as she turned and placed a carved board with oat cakes on it on the table. "Have some," she offered and went to the door.

Saber ignored the cakes and kept his eyes on Elysia, noticing how her hand tightened on the door latch after opening it.

"Clyde. Bliss is not—"

"I know," Clyde said, interrupting her.

Elysia eyed him suspiciously. She did not feel comfortable around Clyde. He had a brash tongue and a manner to match. His solid girth intimidated as did the strength in his thick hands that swung far too quickly when he was the least bit annoyed. His features might have been pleasant if he scowled less. However, he did possess one good habit. He kept himself cleaner than most, no foul order coming from him and he kept his long, dark red hair neatly combed and tethered with a leather tie.

"If you know my sister isn't here, then why are you here?" Elysia asked.

Clyde stepped toward her and she blocked the open door with her body, a warning that he was to go no farther.

Clyde's face pinched in irritation. "I want to talk to you."

Elysia was growing uncomfortable with him. "I have no time to talk with you."

"Make time," he snapped.

Elysia rarely was unkind or rude to anyone, but she felt being blunt with Clyde would be best. "I have no interest in making time for you, Clyde, now leave."

He took a quick step toward her and she jumped back, her eyes turning wide when she felt an arm snag her around the waist and move her aside. The next thing she knew, Saber had Clyde by the throat, forcing him to walk backwards away from the cottage.

Elysia hurried out the door, seeing people already

whispering to one another and pointing toward the two men and her. Worried the scene it created and what might happen between the two men, though she was sure Clyde didn't stand a chance against Saber, she went to stop the incident from turning worse.

Saber's actions brought her to an abrupt halt. He released Clyde with a forcible shove that had the man barely able to remain on his feet and he pointed, as if warning him to leave. Surprisingly, Clyde didn't argue with Saber, though his angry scowl spoke otherwise. He turned and walked off, snapping at people he passed that stared his way.

Elysia was surprised herself when Saber returned to her side, took hold of her arm, and walked with her into the cottage, closing the door behind them. Her worry grew, knowing many had watched and would have something to say to Bliss when she returned.

Once inside, he returned to the chair, sat, and reached for an oat cake as if they had not been disturbed at all.

Elysia was not sure what to say, upset over the incident, and yet words fell easily from her lips. "You protected me. Thank you."

He nodded and his eyes held hers for a moment and though he did not touch her, Elysia felt it more an embrace and a comforting one at that.

She turned away, feeling her cheeks heat with a blush and filled a tankard with the brew. She turned back, now having a plausible excuse for her blossomed red cheeks—the heat from the hearth.

She placed the tankard in front of him and instructed, "Sip slowly so it will soothe your throat."

He nodded, then his head suddenly turned toward the door.

Instinct had Elysia hurrying to stand behind him, worried Clyde had returned, though she had heard no knock.

The door burst opened and Annis rushed in, her face red with rage. "What are you doing to my sister?"

Elysia hurried around to stand protectively in front of Saber. She should have realized someone would have informed her sister about the incident.

"Saber has been kind to me and he protected me from Clyde when he came here with no good intentions and knowing full well I was alone. I was busy seeing to the wound on Saber's finger and preparing a brew for his throat when Clyde showed up. Now please shut the door before all the villagers gather to stare at us."

Annis closed the door and tilted her head to look at Saber. "What is wrong with his throat?"

"He suffered an injury that caused the loss of his voice," Elysia explained and turned to Saber. "Do not let the brew grow cold."

Saber lifted the tankard and sipped.

Annis walked to the other end of the table and stared at Saber. He stared right back at her.

"Thank you for helping my sister," Annis said.

He nodded, pointed to his throat and his finger, then to Annis and then patted his chest.

"You are grateful for her help," Annis said.

He nodded.

"Make sure you behave around my sister," Annis warned.

Saber nodded slowly.

"What have you been up to?" Elysia asked, her eyes traveling over her sister. "Dirt mars a good portion of you."

Annis glanced down at herself, brushing dirt off here and there. "The idiots did not adhere to Duff's instructions on the winter shed. If they had continued to construct it their way, the thing would have collapsed."

"Do not tell me that you demonstrated how their efforts would fail?' Elysia asked with a note of worry.

"What else was I to do? It took nothing more than a bump or two in specific places and the whole thing came tumbling down."

"And covered you in dirt," Elysia reminded.

"A little dirt saved our winter food storage from being ruined," Annis argued. "I have to get back and make sure those idiots build the shed the right way. I rushed here when someone said there was a commotion going on. Duff left me in charge, which is probably why the men started building it their way. They did not think a woman would notice. I showed them how wrong they were." She turned to leave, though swerved around before she reached the door and pointed a threatening finger at Saber. "Mind your manners with my sister or you will answer to me."

Saber nodded, and Annis left in the same rush she had entered.

Elysia turned to Saber worried he might take offense to her sister's threats. "Annis means well, looking after my safety." That a barely detectable smile went along with his nod, vanquished her worries.

He was a fine looking man without a smile, but the slight lift of his mouth made him all the more attractive.

Her stomach fluttered again. She had to stop this nonsense. There were far more important things to concern herself with, and yet this time spent with Saber seemed of the utmost importance. After all, she was helping to heal his throat so his voice would finally return—a voice she could not wait to hear.

***

Bliss always enjoyed time in the woods no matter the season. Spring's new buds reminded that new life was beginning after winter hibernation when all lay quiet in rest, and summer greeted with an abundance of beauty and growth while autumn brought the abundant harvest. The seasons' wisdom and importance was taught to her by Kendesa, the previous clan healer. Its vast knowledge was known to every skilled healer and the seasons reminded when plants should be planted, picked, or left longer to harvest. Kendesa also taught her the importance of respect for the plants, for while they could heal, they could also kill.

It was knowing their properties well that made the difference. And the one person who knew the plants better than anyone was Cumina. She used different plants to make her amulets that were meant to protect people, which meant she had to know something about curses.

Bliss wanted desperately to find a way to break the curse cast on the three men, more so now that she had seen the interest Brogan had in Annis. She truly feared for Annis's fate.

The gray sky overhead hinted at a fall shower, but

then weather was unpredictable in the Highlands—beautiful one moment, gray the next, leaving one to always be cautious as to what garments might be needed.

Raindrops began to fall when she was not far from Cumina's cottage. Bliss hurried her hood over her head and quickened her steps. She was not surprised to see the old woman standing in the open doorway, looking out in wait.

Cumina was often referred to as an old woman, but age had not marred her beauty. She had to be sixty-plus years, and yet her face wore few lines and wrinkles and her bold green eyes were alert and intimidating. She was tall with no stoop to her shoulders that claimed most women with age and she was slim. Her long, pure white hair—she wore in a braid—held a shine that Bliss envied as did she envy the woman's graceful movements—never rushed and always purposeful.

Sometimes Bliss wished she possessed Cumina's magic, not about amulets, but her ability to sense things. Magic most often frightened people and the person thought to possess its strange powers was often avoided, left to live alone away from others and only sought out when in dire need, as Bliss did now.

Cumina waved Bliss forward. "Hurry, the rain will worsen, though it will be gone by the time you leave."

Bliss entered the cottage just as the raindrops turned to a downpour.

"Sit. I have a hot brew for us," Cumina offered, pointing to a chair at a table barely large enough for two.

Bliss pushed her cloak off her shoulders to drape

on the back of the chair. She loved coming here. Cumina's cottage always welcomed and there were so many interesting things to see. A plethora of plants hung on drying racks, crocks sat everywhere, their lids set tight only allowing one to guess what they held, and baskets overflowed with bunches of dried plants, while wrapped herbs hung from pegs on the wall. A well-worn walking stick leaned against the wall near the door. It was made from a sturdy branch of a blackthorn tree which many believed could defend against evil.

"What you ask is not easy," Cumina said, placing a tankard in front of Bliss before joining her at the table, a tankard already waiting there for her.

"You know that I have come to ask about removing a curse," Bliss clarified more for herself than Cumina.

"A powerful curse." Cumina looked down at her tankard a moment, then back at Bliss. "The most powerful curse there is—a death curse. When someone uses their last breath to curse someone, it releases tremendous power. Most times the curse is made because of a wrong that was done to someone and the only way to end the curse is to right the wrong. I know of this curse that was cast on three men and it must be made right to finally end all the sorrow it has caused and will continue to cause."

"I had hoped there was a charm or a magical spell that could break the curse."

"It takes more than a charm or spell to break a curse. It takes an abundance of courage. You must understand that a wrong was done and a wrong often involves evil, and that wrong still exists and doesn't want to be destroyed. It has gained strength through the years and will fight all attempts to extinguish it."

Cumina's warning dashed Bliss's hope of protecting her sisters.

"This is not something that can be done fast. It is something that must be pondered with great care and decided upon with staunch conviction. It is not something to undertake lightly or thought to be done easily."

"But it can be done?" Bliss asked, praying for the answer she wanted to hear.

"As I said, a curse cast by a dying person holds great power. The woman who cast the curse you inquire about did so as she laid dying by her own hand."

"There must be some way," Bliss said, not willing to give up so easily, and seeing the way Cumina eyes briefly avoided hers, she sensed there was a way. "If there is a way, please tell me."

Cumina hesitated.

"Please," Bliss pleaded. "I must protect my sisters."

A sudden awareness sparked in Cumina's eyes. "A promise you made to your mother as she laid dying—to protect your sisters—from the truth." She raised her hand to stop Bliss from responding. "I know not the truth only that you gave your word and that your mother died more peacefully for it. I warn you, though, a death promise can be a heavy burden and your mother would relieve you of it if the day should ever come that you must break your word to her."

"I carry it without burden," Bliss said.

"A secret is always a burden," Cumina gently advised.

Bliss did not want to hear any more about the promise she had made her mum. It was done and the secret would be kept.

"Please tell me if there is a way to break the curse," Bliss pleaded, returning to the reason of why she was there.

Cumina relented. "The witch of the hills would know how to break the curse."

"I thought the witch of the hills was nothing more than a myth that had grown through the ages," Bliss said.

"I can assure you the witch of the hills is no myth, and her power has grown through the years and some believe it is more evil than good."

"If there is a chance, I must try," Bliss said.

"In saving your sisters, you may lose yourself. The witch of the hills demands a price for her magic. Will you be willing to pay that price?"

Chapter Six

Annis tried to temper her anger. She had thought Duff not only a good man but a friend. He had taught her much when it came to building structures and there was so much more she wished to learn, but no more according to Duff. The men she had made to look like fools had complained to Duff and he told her that she could no longer work with him. The men had told him they would not work with her. So it was her or them and she could easily be spared, not so the men.

She walked through the village trying to ignore the whispers and snickers that followed her. She did not need to hear what they were saying, she knew. The men thought her a fool for thinking she had the intelligence to do a man's task and the women thought her foolish for even wanting to do a man's task. She had been interested in how things were constructed since she had been young. She had built things out of twigs and branches, mud and clay, and whatever else she could find since her hands could first grasp something.

Duff had entertained her with stories of how some of his ancestors helped build Edinburgh Castle. She had been enthralled by the stories of how it was built atop of a rock, a solid structure that could withstand any attack. She could only imagine the design and talent that went into building such a marvel.

She would probably never see it, but she hoped one

day to design and build not such a grand structure, but a good solid one for her and her sisters. One that would have more than one room to it.

"You look like you have rolled in the dirt."

"Better than bruised and battered," Annis snapped, recognizing Brogan's voice but not bothering to look his way.

"A spark of anger to your words," Brogan said. "Who got you so riled up?"

"It does not concern you," Annis said annoyed, seeing their conversation was drawing attention, which was not a good thing. She wanted nothing to do with Brogan and she definitely did not want to be considered as a possible wife for him. She would kill him first.

"It does if I ask," he said with a command that brought Annis to a halt.

She turned to face him and was caught by his features that were much too handsome for a man and that she even thought that annoyed her all the more.

She planted her hands on her hips and shot Brogan an intense glare that often withered a man. "So you order me to tell you when I care not to speak with you?"

He smiled and she heard the gasps that circulated around them, though she did not join in. His smile might heighten his fine features, but she did not give a fig.

"Why not speak with me? I thought our last talk was quite invigorating."

That sent tongues wagging and Annis feared she was making it worse for herself. She could almost hear Bliss warning her to walk away and not engage the man. Unfortunately, it was not in her nature.

"Maddening, it was just that—nothing more than maddening," she corrected.

Brogan laughed. "I thought it delightful, but we digress. Where did all the dirt come from?" He waved his hand up from her feet to the top of her head to remind her of his inquiry.

She had no wont to answer him, but feared the conversation would remain never-ending if she did not. "A mishap."

His smile vanished when he hastily asked, "You were not hurt, were you?"

Annis threw her arms wide. "Do I look hurt?"

His smile quickly returned. "No, not at all. You are still a ravishing beauty even with all the dirt on you."

That really got whispers circulating and got Annis on the verge of losing her temper.

"Maybe your sweet talk works on other women, but it is lost on me. You are nothing more than an annoying fool to me." That got a ton of gasps and more people stopping to watch them.

"Ouch! That hurt," Brogan said with a laugh.

"Good, then it did what I intended. Now take yourself off and find a willing lass to cool your ardor." Loud gasps warned her that she may have crossed a line.

Brogan stepped closer to her and, of course, she held her ground, not daring to show a pinch of intimidation even if there was a little.

Brogan lowered his head and kept his voice low. "I do not take well to orders, lass, and when I see something I want, I make sure I get it."

Her mind warned her but the anger that had her stomach churning won out and her finger lashed out to poke him in the chest. "I do not take well to orders from men who think to force themselves on me."

"I do not force women. They invite me."

Annis jabbed him in the chest again. "Then let me settle this. I will NEVER—I repeat so you hear me clearly—I will NEVER invite you to poke me."

Brogan grinned. "Mind your words, lass, especially the word never. It has a way of coming back to bite you."

"Never! Never! Never!" she spat with each poke. A sharp command had Annis jumping.

"You do not touch Lord Brogan without permission!"

She dropped her finger off Brogan and looked to see Cadell.

"You will be punished for that," Cadell threatened.

"NO SHE WILL NOT!" Brogan ordered with such a strong command that it had Annis turning to see if it had truly been him who had spoken. "If I hear of Annis suffering any punishment, you will receive a worst one. Do I make myself clear, Cadell?"

"Aye, my lord," Cadell said wisely, though with a bit of anger.

Brogan presented his back to Cadell, blocking Annis from his view. "You intrigue me, Annis. Come sup with me at the keep tonight so we may talk."

Her response was swift. "No."

"That is it, no?" Brogan asked, shaking his head. "You offer no reason."

"I do not want to sup with you," she clarified.

"Now I must be on my way." She turned to leave and caught Cadell's words.

"Order her to sup with you."

That had Annis turning back around. "Lord Brogan, a word?"

He went to her, a gleam in his eyes that she may have changed her mind.

Annis kept her voice to a whisper. "Do you wish to wed me?"

The gleam left Brogan's eyes. "I would not condemn you to such a hell."

"What do you think will happen if you continue to show interest in me?" she asked.

His eyes went wide, then they narrowed, a hint of a glare in them. "You are right and I will trouble you no more."

Annis did not expect to feel sorry for the man, but at that moment she suffered a jab to her heart and got the sense she felt his loneliness. It was a deep, all-consuming emptiness that terrified her. She would never want to feel that way. She almost called out to him, wanting to offer him at least friendship, but she did not dare. The consequences were far too dangerous.

He walked off, not saying another word. She did not doubt he would keep his word, but one look at Cadell told a different tale. And the way he grinned at her and scurried off, she was certain he was going to find Lawler and report what had gone on between her and Brogan. What then? Would the decision be taken from Brogan? Had she placed herself in a precarious situation?

She ignored the whispers and stares as she made

her way home. Bliss had to be told what she had done, told of her foolishness. She hoped nothing would come of it, but something warned her otherwise.

Annis entered the cottage, ready to confess all until she saw the look of despair on her sisters' faces. "Tell me," she said, fearful of the news.

Bliss detailed her visit to Cumina.

"That does it. You are not going to the witch in the hills for help," Annis ordered when Bliss finished. "There is no telling what she will want from you in return for her help. You will not take such a dangerous chance."

"I agree with Annis," Elysia said. "Besides, we may be spared being chosen, then there will be no need for worry. No attention has been paid to me or Bliss. You, Annis," —Elysia shook her finger at her— "need to stay out of Lord Brogan's sight."

Annis scrunched her face. "I had a slight problem with that today."

Bliss gripped her chest, a pain of worry squeezing at her. "What happened?"

"Lord Brogan and I shared a few words, but I asked him if he wished to wed me—"

"What?" Bliss and Elysia said in unison.

"Do not get upset. I purposely asked him to remind him that his interest in me could very well earn him a wife... a wife he did not want. He agreed and told me he would not trouble me again," Annis explained and lowered her head, her eyes unable to meet her sisters'.

"What are you not telling us?" Bliss asked, worry gripping stronger at her heart.

Annis looked from one sister to the other. "The

man with Lawler… Cadell. He witnessed our exchange, but I do not believe he heard what I asked Brogan about marrying me."

"Good God," Bliss said and dropped down on one of the three chairs at the table.

"Something else you should know. Duff told me I cannot work with him any longer. The men complained that I purposely made them look like fools and they refuse to have me around," Annis said and dropped down on one of the other chairs, upset over losing the work she so enjoyed.

Bliss reached out and laid her hand over Annis's, giving it a comforting squeeze. "I am so sorry, Annis. I know how much that work meant to you, not to mention Duff's friendship."

"He will not even want to be seen with me now, for fear of what the men will think. I do not know what I am going to do. The chieftain will make sure I am given a woman's chore and I will go completely mad."

"I should mention what happened to me today," Elysia said, joining her sisters at the table.

Bliss's worry mounted.

"Clyde came here knowing full well you were not here—to talk to me, so he said. He would have forced his way into the cottage if it had not been for Saber. He grabbed Clyde by the throat and made it clear by his actions alone that he was to leave and not return. Then Saber escorted me back inside. I had fixed him a brew for his throat to help him regain his voice, and he sat for some time drinking it. I also had him take s spoonful of the bramble berry syrup, then I encouraged him to return each day to take both in hopes that it will heal his throat and restore his voice."

Bliss rubbed her brow, a dull ache starting.

"Tongues will wag about that, but Saber does seem a good man."

Elysia was quick to defend him. "He is and well-mannered when with me."

"You favor Saber," Annis said with a teasing smile.

"Do you, Elysia?" Bliss asked, pleased that at least one of them might have found favor with a good man.

Elysia blushed, which of course had Annis teasing her all the more.

"Your cheeks bloom red. Goodness, you do like him." Annis kept her grin but pointed an accusing finger at Elysia. "But is he not too big for you? Would he not squash you in bed?"

"Annis!" Bliss scolded.

Elysia's blush deepened. "Though large in size, he seems a kind man."

"And he is quiet," Annis said, trying to hide her laugh.

"Annis," Bliss scolded again. "That is not nice to say when you know he has lost his voice."

"Well that does work for Elysia. She prefers quiet, and what is better than a husband who cannot complain or yell at his wife?"

Bliss and Elysia could not help but laugh.

"I believe there are many women who would agree with you," Bliss said.

"I would not mind hearing his voice. I believe it would be gentle and not booming or commanding like many men," Elysia said, a soft dreamy smile on her face.

"Be careful, Elysia," Annis warned. "Not everyone is who they first seem. I thought Duff was a friend, but he quickly discarded me rather than defend me."

"I truly am sorry for you, Annis," Elysia said. "I will tell the chieftain that I will teach you how to stitch."

"He will laugh at you, as will others," Annis said. "And no one will bring their stitching to you, for fear I will have a hand in it."

"Who then will they bring it to that does such as fine of a job as I do?" Elysia asked with pride in her work.

"You are right about that," Annis agreed.

"It does not matter. It will be nothing more than a ruse for you to have time to see what else may fit you better."

"That is a good idea, Elysia," Bliss said, Elysia usually being too honest and kind to suggest a ruse, though it seemed not when it came to helping her sister.

"I truly appreciate that, Elysia. It chases some of my worry away," Annis said.

"It also gives you a reason to remain in the cottage, at least until Lord Brogan takes his leave," Bliss said with some relief.

"I hope he leaves soon," Annis complained. "I will not be able to remain cooped up in the cottage for long or I will go mad."

"We can always take a wander in the woods to search for animal bones to make more needles," Elysia suggested.

"That I will gladly do, since I do enjoy making

your needles," Annis said.

"Then things are settled for now and we should enjoy supper, freshly baked bannock and cabbage soup," Bliss said.

"Sit," Elysia ordered gently. "I made it and I will serve it."

A knock sounded at the door and it opened before Bliss could question who was there.

Lawler rushed in and looked to Bliss. "A dispute at the keep, you are needed to tend someone."

Bliss nodded, not saying another word, eager to hurry and fetch her healing basket.

"Annis will come too," Lawler ordered.

"Why?" Bliss demanded more strongly than she intended.

"You do not question me, woman. You do as you are told," Lawler commanded.

"Annis faints at the sight of blood," Elysia said in an effort to protect her sister. "I can help Bliss."

"I will not repeat myself. Bliss and Annis will do as they are told," Lawler said, leaving no room to argue.

Bliss kept her voice to a whisper as she and Annis followed behind Lawler to the keep. "You will say nothing—not a word. Heed me on this, Annis. And heed your temper, for it may cost you if you do not."

Annis nodded, clamping her lips tightly shut in preparation and fighting to tamp down the annoyance that repeatedly poked at her. She recalled her mum telling her more often than not that she should have been born into royalty since she obeyed no one and did as she pleased.

Bliss and Annis both came to an abrupt halt when they entered the Great Hall. Food lay scattered about from an overturned table, and Chieftain Emory stood between Lord Brogan and Cadell as servants scurried around the two men to clean up the mess.

"You make no decisions for me, Cadell," Brogan yelled, shaking his fist at the man.

"I take orders from your father, not you," Cadell shot back.

Brogan caught sight of Annis and Bliss and fury sparked in his eyes. "What is she doing here?" Cadell went to turn and Brogan hurried in front of him. He was quick to look to Bliss. "Cadell is bleeding badly."

Bliss hurried to stand in front of her sister.

Brogan shook his fist at Lawler. "You had no right to bring Annis here."

"Your father's orders take precedent," Lawler said.

"There is nothing I favor about Annis, nothing. She is annoying, pays no mind to my word, and I have no desire to bed her and never will. Even worse, she faints at the sight of too much blood, something that can often be found on me. And must I remind you again that I want no wife?"

"And must I remind you that your father has instructed that you will wed," Lawler said as if tired of reminding him. "Would it not be better that you favor the woman you wed, rather than be stuck with one you have no like for at all?"

Brogan ignored Lawler and called out, "Annis, you will return home now."

Bliss stepped aside ready to hurry her sister out, but Cadell was quicker. He stepped around Brogan and caught Annis's eye.

Annis caught one look of the blood running down his nose and from his lip, covering a good portion of his chin, and paled. Try as she might she could not fight it.

Brogan let an oath fly as he rushed to Annis, catching her before she hit the floor.

Bliss did not miss the look Cadell exchanged with Lawler. His quick action proved what they both thought—Brogan favored Annis. Bliss thought she might faint as well, but kept her sense about her.

Brogan sat on the one bench that had been left standing when the table in front of it had been toppled. He cradled Annis in his arms, resting her comfortably in his lap. He sent a worried look to Bliss.

Bliss wished there was someplace Brogan could set her down, but there was nothing suitable and she had no choice but to tell him, "Keep hold of her until she comes to."

He nodded and turned his eyes on Annis. Her beauty could not be denied, but beauty could be deceiving. It was her bold, clever tongue that challenged and had him smiling more often than not. And damn if he did not want to run his hands through her flaming red hair that burst in ringlets around her head as wildly and uncontrollably as her words that often burst from her lips. Lips that appeared far too delectable.

Bliss's stomach roiled seeing the intense interest in Brogan's eyes for her sister. This was not good, not good at all. He might protest that he did not favor Annis, but it was obvious he lied. He very much favored Annis.

She had to get Annis out of there as soon as possible, though she wondered if it was too late. Had her sister's fate already been sealed?

"Let me see to your wounds," Bliss said, turning to Cadell.

He nodded and sat on a bench at a table that had not been overturned.

Bliss prayed that Annis's faint would last until she was done with Cadell. She feared what her words would be when she woke and found herself in Brogan's arms. She kept a litany of silent prayers going as she hurried to clean Cadell's wounds.

Chapter Seven

Brogan was relieved when Annis finally stirred in his arms, though disappointed as well since she would not remain in his arms long. Strange how much he enjoyed holding her.

Let her go!

The warning rang clear in his head. He could not condemn her to a life with him. It was not fair to either of them, but more so to her.

Her eyes began to flutter and he could not help but smile and wonder over her reaction when she looked upon his face. He was caught by surprise when her eyes opened and she smiled at him... though not for long.

"Let go of me," she ordered like one who was used to issuing such demands and having them obeyed.

"You think I want to hold you?" he sneered, though laughed. "I should have let you hit the floor when you fainted."

"It would have been preferable to your arms," Annis shot back.

He wanted to laugh again and tease her so she would verbally spar with him, but his warning rang in his head again.

Let her go!

He paid heed and eased her off his lap, keeping his hands at her waist to make sure she remained steady on her feet.

Annis was about to pull away from him when a shock of lightheadedness hit as it usually did after coming to from a faint, and she was glad for the hold he had on her.

He held her firm, feeling her unsteady on her feet and that she did not protest confirmed his concern. It was not long before she found firm footing and though he did not release her, he was quick to order, "Go home, I have no need of you now or ever."

Annis pulled away from him and gave no thought to her tongue. "And you think I have need of you?"

"Maybe not need, but desire is something most women cannot control around me." He grinned dismissively. "But know full well that I have no desire to poke you."

Annis's face turned red with fury. "Like I would let you? I would see you dead first."

"ENOUGH!" Lawler shouted. "How dare you threaten Lord Brogan."

"Keep her from me, Lawler, or else she may do what others have failed to do… see me dead," Brogan said and walked away from Annis.

"I am finished," Bliss said. "Your nose is not broken and your lip will heal in time." Hasty steps had her beside her sister. "We will take our leave."

"If Annis threatens Lord Brogan again, she will be punished," Lawler warned.

"I will make certain she keeps her distance," Bliss said with a respectful bob of her head.

"See that you do," Lawler ordered and snapped his hand at a servant to show the two women out.

"Can you believe Lord Brogan's audacity?" Annis

asked, shaking her head as Bliss hurried her through the village.

"Your temper gets in the way of the truth," Bliss chastised.

Annis turned a puzzled look on her sister. "What do you mean?"

"Do you not realize what Lord Brogan did for you?"

"He insulted me," Annis argued.

"He was protecting you," Bliss corrected.

Annis went to argue and stopped.

"He said what he did to protect you," Bliss said. "He kept his word about troubling you no more. He made sure you would not be chosen as his wife. He is an honorable man."

Annis hurried her steps to keep up with Bliss, her remark having slowed them. She had much to consider and was annoyed with herself for not seeing what had been obvious.

"I believe Lord Brogan counted on your quick tongue to help him and you did not fail him," Bliss said, grateful to him for what he had done. "You will mind your tongue and yourself until Lawler and Cadell take their leave."

"How can a man be such an arse and gallant at the same time?" Annis asked, shaking her head.

"Perhaps it is because he knows what it is to be condemned and does not wish it on another."

Bliss's words turned Annis quiet, a miracle in itself. Annis could not fathom being condemned to be Lord Brogan's wife. It would be unthinkable. She did not like feeling grateful to the man, but begrudgingly she did. She also continued to feel sorry for him and the loneliness the curse forced him to endure. Still, she would be glad to see him take his leave of the village—posthaste.

***

"Gather the larger bones," Elysia instructed as she walked with Annis through the woods.

"I will gather various bones so that I can try making different size needles than you already have," Annis said, looking forward to the task.

"That would be wonderful. I would like some different sizes to see what I could do with them," Elysia encouraged. "It is good you are here in the woods away from the village where gossip abounds about you."

"There are some tongues wagging about you too," Annis accused.

"Few compared to you," Elysia said and, stopped walking, forcing Annis to do the same. "It is punishment I fear for you, Annis. The men talk of your interference with building the food shed when if it was not for you the village would have lost all that would have been stored in it, but the men refuse to admit the truth. Then to make matters worse, you spoke brazenly to Lord Brogan causing fear of retribution by his father. Even Lord Emory has been heard offering his apology to Lord Brogan the last couple of days following the incident at the keep. You have stirred the cauldron considerably and, in doing so, have left few who would defend you."

"I have done what Bliss asked and have kept to the

cottage. What more can I do?" Annis asked, guilt plaguing her.

Elysia laid a comforting hand on her sister's shoulder. "Something most difficult for you—have patience and let this pass. Some other gossip will soon replace it and no longer will anyone pay you heed. Put your mind to the task at hand and let your worry fade for a while."

Annis nodded. She missed working with Duff, but there was little she could do about that now. She supposed if she had handled the incident with the men differently, perhaps made it look as if one of the men had realized the mistake to the structure, then all would have turned out well. In time, perhaps they would have accepted the fact that, woman or not, she had the knowledge to build structures as well as a man.

"Enough, Annis," she quietly warned herself. She was here to help her sister and, if anything, she always made sure to complete whatever task given her. And it was kind of Elysia to help her so she would not have to suffer at a woman's task she most certainly would hate.

With her mind finally set on the task at hand, she combed the area for animal bones. She collected a few and turned to show her sister a specific one that she felt would make a good thick needle to stitch hides. Elysia was nowhere in sight. She had wandered farther from her sister than she had realized.

"What are you doing out here alone?"

The sharp chastising voice had her turning with a flourish to face Brogan. "I am with my sister, not that it is any concern of yours."

Brogan continued to scold. "I do not see her and

that matters not. Neither of you should be in the woods alone."

Annis pasted a forced smile on her face. "I will consider your advice."

"It is an order, not advice, and you will adhere to it," Brogan commanded curtly, annoyed that her smile flared his desire. He really needed to find himself a willing woman and ease his need.

Annis went to step forward and argue with him and caught herself. She had to hold her tongue no matter how difficult.

"I'll find my sister and return to the village," she said and went to turn away.

"Now see, it was not that difficult to obey my word," he said, a teasing chuckle highlighting his remark.

She warned herself to leave, keep hold of her tongue, not look back, but unfortunately she did not pay heed to her own warning. She turned to look at him and once she saw that smug smirk on his face, her tongue slipped away from her. "Obey? You actually think I intend to obey you? You are more a fool than I thought." Anger flared in her eyes when he laughed.

"I could not help myself. You are so easily teased, and I so enjoy the challenge you present," he said, fighting not to laugh. "Though I should remind you that if we were not alone you would find yourself in trouble for calling me a fool."

"And here I thought it was something you heard often," Annis said with a sweet smile.

Brogan let some laughter slip. "Thought by many I'm sure, but none say it to my face, except for my father, of course. He reminds me often that I am a fool."

The thought that his father could be so cruel when the fault was his own for what Brogan suffered had her defending him. "Your father is more the fool for bringing the curse down on you."

Brogan's smile vanished. "Never speak about the curse. I will not have you touched by its horror."

With his smile gone and the intensity of his words, Annis got a peek at a different man. A man who would let no one get the least bit close, a man who was more alone than anyone could ever imagine and to even imagine such loneliness troubled her heart. It was not right. Brogan had done nothing wrong, his father had and he should be the one to bear the burden, not his son.

She thought about the witch in the hills. "What if there was a way to break the curse?"

"There isn't," he said, warning himself not to discuss it any further with her, but for some strange reason unable to resist doing so. "I have searched endlessly for a solution only reaching the same conclusion over and over—the curse cannot be broken. It must be fulfilled and that is impossible to do."

"What do you mean?" Annis asked curious, not having heard that.

His tongue was curt. "I will talk of it no more with you."

Annis would not be dismissed or dissuaded. "You throw away any chance of finding a solution if you refuse to talk of what you know, hear what others may know, and come away with more knowledge because of it."

"Rannick thought that and lost three wives and a

bairn. He has traveled to foreign lands searching for the magic that could right this terrible wrong and has returned—" Brogan shook his head. "He is more animal than man now, no one able to go near him. His father keeps him locked away, for fear of what he might do to others."

"Why then does Lord Lochlann search for a wife for his son if he is barely human?" Annis asked, a shiver of fear rising gooseflesh along her arms. She shook her head, recalling what she had heard. "I forgot. An heir. It is because Lord Lochlann is determined to have an heir to the Clan MacClaren."

"He does. Whereas Rannick refuses to father any children and have them suffer the horrors he has. He wants to see the MacClaren bloodline brought to an end."

"And do you want that as well?" Annis asked.

It took a moment for Brogan to respond. "It is the only way to end the curse."

His moment of pause made Annis believe it was not truly what he wanted and she offered what might be of help to him. "There is the witch in the hills that may be of help."

Brogan shook his head. "She is nothing more than a myth. I should know, since I have searched for her."

"Maybe you did not search in the right place."

Brogan's smile returned. "You suggest I do not know what I am doing?" He laughed. "You do enjoy insulting me, don't you?"

Annis grinned. "It has its moments, and in this case, I would suggest you take another look. You do not know what you might have missed."

"Annis!"

Annis cringed and Brogan chuckled as she turned to face her sister.

"What are you doing?" Elysia demanded, hurrying toward her. "I am sorry, Lord Brogan, for anything my sister may have said to offend you. Please forgive her."

"Forgive me for what?" Annis demanded. "I did nothing to offend him. His own words manage to do that on their own."

"ANNIS!" Elysia scolded.

Brogan laughed. "Has your sister always had a difficult time controlling her tongue?"

"As long as I can remember. Please, do forgive her," Elysia pleaded.

"Forgive me? I did nothing wrong," Annis insisted.

"Worry not, I forgive her foolish tongue," Brogan said with a smirk he knew would get a response.

"Foolish tongue?" Annis snapped and her eyes narrowed in an angry glare that only made him laugh harder. "I would keep those lips locked good or else all will see who has a foolish tongue."

Brogan took a quick step toward her and was not surprised that her chin went up defiantly. He was so close to her that the fiery green color of her eyes drew him in, holding him captive. It took a moment for him to escape their intensity and say, "Then seal my lips shut good—with a kiss."

He heard Elysia gasp, but not Annis. Her chin went up higher and she tilted her head back as if she was about to reach up and kiss him and like a fool he lowered his head.

She smiled sweetly, her warm breath whispering

across his lips as she said, "You will have your kiss, Lord Brogan—" Her hand shot out with such speed to jab him in the stomach that he stumbled back a step. "In your dreams, for never ever will I kiss you." She turned. "Come on, Elysia, and do not dare apologize to him."

Elysia hurried along with her sister, upset at the intense glare she had seen in Lord Brogan's eyes.

***

"No one saw us, so there is no reason to worry," Annis said that night as she and her sisters prepared for bed.

"And how do you know for sure that no one saw you in the woods with Lord Brogan?" Bliss asked, arranging her sleeping pallet on the floor as she did each night, the bed too small to hold more than two people.

Annis had no answer for her.

"It is how you spoke to Lord Brogan that worries me. He protected you the other day—"

"Yet he sees me in the woods and talks to me when he vowed to keep his distance," Annis reminded.

Bliss rubbed her head, an ache having started and grown as Elysia told her about the incident in the woods. Both sisters had waited to seek their beds until she returned home late from delivering a bairn.

"This must stop, Annis, or you could very well be forced to wed Lord Brogan." Bliss turned a warning scowl on her when she went to argue. "Understand that no matter how much you might protest or threaten, you would be forced to wed Lord Brogan and be taken from Elysia and me."

"I am sorry," Annis said. "It is difficult to hold my tongue around Lord Brogan. I think he enjoys teasing me."

Bliss rubbed her head again, the ache not easing. "And if Lawler or Cadell sees that, they will be sure to know he is interested in you and tell Lord Brogan's father who will force a marriage between you both, whether either one of you want it or not."

"I will stay in the cottage until—"

"No," Bliss said. "I realized that would seem like we are hiding you. Avoid Lord Brogan if you can, but most importantly hold your tongue no matter what. Lendra told me that Lawler and Cadell will be leaving soon. She heard them talk about visiting another clan. They want Lord Brogan to go with them, but he has not said if he would yet. They also talked about their worry in finding Lord Rannick a wife. They feel there is no one brave enough to deal with him."

"They are probably right from what Lord Brogan told me about him," Annis said.

"What did he tell you?" Elysia asked.

"That Lord Rannick is more animal than man from losing three wives and a bairn to the curse and his ventures on foreign soil to find the magic to break the curse only made it worse. He is kept locked away by his father for fear of what his son may do to others. Lord Rannick refuses to have any bairns, which must infuriate his father. He wants the Clan MacClaren's bloodline to die off so that no more are forced to live the horror that he does."

"How awful for him," Elysia said.

"I told Lord Brogan about the witch in the hills and he told me she's a myth, that he had searched for her and never found her." Annis's brow narrowed. "He said something strange. He told me he searched endlessly for a way to end the curse and reached the same conclusion over and over—the curse could not be broken. It had to be fulfilled and he said that was impossible to do."

"He did not say why it was impossible?" Bliss asked.

Annis shook her head.

"Getting little sleep tonight will not help us when the day dawns tomorrow," Bliss said, shooing her sisters to the bed.

"We must be hopeful that Lawler, Cadell, and Lord Brogan take their leave soon so this will finally be done," Elysia said.

"We can only pray," Bliss said as she settled on her pallet for the night, but something told her this was not finished and she feared it would not end well.

Chapter Eight

It was market day in the village and to Bliss's surprise, it was crowded. No longer did mothers hide their daughters away and that thought alarmed her. It could only mean one of two things. That Lawler and Cadell had taken their leave, or a woman had been chosen for Lord Brogan.

Bliss's gait turned purposeful. She had to find Lendra and find out what she knew. Though the sun shined bright and smiles and chatter abounded, Bliss felt a worry in the pit of her stomach. She was relieved to see Lendra a short distance ahead. As if the woman sensed her near, she turned and the dire look on her face sent a tremble through Bliss.

"Tell me," Bliss urged when she reached Lendra and the woman hustled them off to a spot that afforded them privacy.

"Tongues run rampant with news that a woman has been chosen for Lord Brogan," Lendra said and shook her head. "I cannot confirm or deny it, since no one in the keep has heard such news."

"A rumor perhaps?" Bliss suggested, praying it was so.

"I suppose it is possible." Lendra squeezed Bliss's hand. "I can tell you that Lord Brogan was heard arguing with Lawler and Cadell last night, though no one heard what it was about. The servants keep a distance from Lord Brogan, fearful of somehow being touched by his curse."

"I heard Lawler and Cadell were to leave soon and visit another clan," Bliss said, wishing to hear it was so.

"There are many things being said and I wonder if it is on purpose so no one knows the truth until it is revealed."

"I worry for Annis," Bliss confessed.

"And well you should. Many believe if anyone is chosen to be Lord Brogan's wife, it will be Annis." Lendra looked around before whispering, "I did hear that Lawler believes Annis would make the cursed lord a good wife since she is so fearless."

Bliss's hand went to her chest. "Good Lord, what am I to do?"

Tears gathered in Lendra's eyes. "Nothing. You can do nothing, none of us can." She nodded toward the crowd. "Though it seems most believe the deed has been done, but only time will tell."

Bliss wandered through the market, keeping a smile on her face, while worry churned her stomach. After talking and laughing with a few merchants who had brought their wares there to sell, she realized smiles were less abundant. Most had thought the choice had been made, but now seeing that Bliss was her usual self, they had begun to wonder. Surely, if Annis had been chosen to be Lord Brogan's wife, Bliss would not be her usual pleasant self.

It took every ounce of strength Bliss had not to hurry through the market. She wanted nothing more than to take herself off somewhere where she could think and plan what could be done if such a fate befell

Annis.

Lendra might believe there was nothing that could be done to save Annis, but Bliss didn't believe that. Unfortunately, there was no time to go search and seek help from the witch in the hills or try to learn what Lord Brogan meant when he told Annis that the curse could not be broken that it had to be fulfilled and how that was impossible to do. What then was left to her?

***

Elysia stood outside the cottage, looking to the woods. It was her fault Annis had gone off alone. With all that had happened yesterday, she had not realized that Annis had not collected any bones and had mentioned it to her. Annis had given pause, then shook her head, realizing she had dropped them during her altercation with Lord Brogan. She insisted on returning to the woods to retrieve her bundle of bones.

Unfortunately, Elysia could not go with her. She had given Bliss her word to remain at the cottage while she went to market in case anyone came in need of healing. Maybe Bliss thought that Annis need not remain confined to the cottage, but Elysia was worried having seen the exchange between Annis and Lord Brogan. She could not get that intense look in Lord Brogan's eyes, after his confrontation with Annis, out of her thoughts. There was something about it that concerned her. Having thought on it, she realized the intensity in his eyes had not been anger. And while she had never seen passion spark in a man's eyes, she had heard women speak about it, some good, some not. She had come to the conclusion that was what she had seen in Lord Brogan's eyes for Annis—passion. And that truly worried her.

"The voiceless fella not here to defend you today?"

A spark of dread ran through Elysia upon hearing Clyde's voice. She turned, glad she stood a distance from the cottage's open door. At least, he couldn't push her inside and shut the door.

"What do you want, Clyde?" she asked, never feeling comfortable around a man of solid girth since she was petite and did not have the strength to defend against him. Not so Saber, and that continued to surprise her.

He raised his hand, holding out one finger. "Cut myself."

Elysia did not see any blood from where she stood and that worried her even more. "Sit down at the table," she instructed with a nod to the small table and two benches Bliss kept outside. There were some men Bliss refused to tend in the cottage and having shared her concern with Chieftain Emory, he had agreed with her, hence the table and benches outside.

"You'll tend me inside," he ordered gruffly.

"I will tend you outside or not at all," Elysia said, wishing one of her sisters would hurry and return.

Clyde scowled. "You tend Saber inside."

She refused to argue with him and repeated, "Outside or not at all."

"You need a husband who will teach you how to keep a civil tongue with a man," he said with a snarl that curled his upper lip.

His snarl, far too similar to that of a dog about to

attack, had her crossing her arms over her chest in hopes it would distract from the shiver that ran through her. "Since you find me uncivil, it would be best if Bliss tended your wound."

"I'll have you tend it, not your sister," he ordered and took a step toward her.

"Elysia is not a healer, I am."

Clyde turned to see Bliss walking toward him.

"Now sit down and behave or I will report your rude manner to the chieftain," Bliss ordered, pointing to the benches.

"I can see to it myself," Clyde snapped and pointed his finger at Elysia. "Hear this well. No man wants anything to do with either of you because of that crazy sister of yours. You'll come begging me to marry Elysia and by then it might be too late."

Bliss went to her sister as Clyde walked off and slipped her arm around her. "While I don't wish Clyde on any poor woman, I do hope his warning proves true so that he leaves you alone."

Elysia gripped Bliss's arm. "Don't tell, Annis. It will upset her."

Bliss shook her head. "I was about to warn you of the same, though she would be angrier rather than upset and she would no doubt pay Clyde a visit."

"Only worsening her situation," Elysia said.

"I fear her situation has grown far worse. Come inside and I will tell you what I have heard."

***

Annis was glad for an excuse to return to the

woods. It was quiet there and a place where she could think and use the stones, twigs, dirt, and whatever else might help her build various small structures to see how they would go together to learn what worked and what didn't.

Unfortunately, today wasn't a day she could linger. She had promised Elysia she would not take long. She would find the bones she had dropped and hurry back. She had forgotten all about the bones she had collected for her sister. She could not even say when they had fallen from her hand, Brogan had annoyed her so badly.

She stopped walking. Why she found it so natural to refer to him by his name and not his title was a mystery to her. She had to catch herself to address him properly in front of others and yet when alone with him, his name was all that fell from her lips.

Lips.

She got annoyed recalling how close she had come to kissing him or that she had even given it thought. Or that his lips had enticed. She had never given thought to kiss any man. She cringed at the thought. But why hadn't she cringed at the thought of kissing Brogan?

She couldn't deny he was an attractive man, pleasant to look upon and not bad to talk with even though he teased her. She did feel sorry for what he had had to endure and it continued to anger her that his father thought him a fool when his lot in life had been caused by the man. Still, none of that was any reason to kiss Brogan. So why had she felt an urge to kiss him?

"The better question," she asked herself, "is why you should be wasting your thoughts on such nonsense?"

She shook her head, clearing it, and made her way to the spot where she thought she had dropped the bones. It took a bit of searching but she finally found them. She scooped them up and was about to turn when she thought she heard footfalls and the rustle of branches.

Annis ducked down quickly behind a tree and slowly glanced a peek around it. She caught a flash of movement, a cloak if she was not mistaken, and watched as it appeared again through the trees, then it stopped suddenly. Had the person heard her? Fear tingled along her spine. Brogan was right, the woods could prove dangerous, especially when spying on someone.

She remained as still as she could and the figure moved again and stopped after only a few steps. He turned then, his face peeking out from the hood of his cloak.

Brogan.

Why was he here again, in nearly the same spot as they were the other day? She got her answer when she heard another set of footfalls. He was meeting someone. Had that been why he had been here the other day? Had he come to meet someone? Had she interrupted his meeting?

She did not dare try and get any closer for fear of being heard and caught and if it were only Brogan, she wouldn't care. But she did not know who the other person was and that could prove dangerous.

The woods carried sound easily and she listened for their voices to drift to her. She only got bits and pieces, the distance making it difficult to recognize the

voices.
"Nothing."
"Disappointed again."
"Must try."
"No choice."
"No time."
"Not just you."
"End it otherwise."

A flock of birds burst from some of the treetops, startling Annis and the two men sensed it could very well signal that someone approached. She could not hear the last few words they exchanged before they fled in opposite directions. She waited to make sure neither of them lingered about before she crept away as quietly as she could. She picked up speed once she got close to the village and burst into the cottage to find her sisters sitting at the table, worry heavy on their faces.

"What now?" Annis asked, annoyed that life had turned so difficult so rapidly, and joined them at the table.

"Tongues wag that a wife has been chosen for Lord Brogan," Bliss said.

"Is there proof to these rumors?" Annis asked, fearing she had sealed her own fate. "I thought Lawler and Cadell were leaving to go to another clan."

"So it was believed, but now tongues wag otherwise," Bliss said.

"Then what truly is the truth?" Annis asked, hoping it was nothing more than gossip, something villagers loved to spread.

"I do not know," Bliss said, feeling more helpless than she ever had. "But I do worry."

"What are we to do if it is true?" Elysia asked.

"I assume you believe that I have been chosen to be Lord Brogan's wife," Annis said, unfortunately, thinking the same herself.

"It would seem likely," Elysia admitted, wishing it was not so.

"Then there is little we can do." Annis did not want to believe her own words.

"Our worry could all be for naught," Bliss said and saw on their grim faces that none of them believed that. "I will think of something," she assured her sisters.

"I know you hope to," Annis said, "but there is little chance of that now. And from what I just heard in the woods, there is little chance of being rid of this curse that has troubled so many."

"What do you mean?" Elysia asked.

"I hid while Brogan met with another man and could hear only snippets of their conversation," Annis explained. "From what I could gather they were disappointed again and time was not on their side. I imagine they referred to whatever it was they search for, and I can only assume it has something to do with what Brogan said about the curse being fulfilled yet him thinking it impossible."

Elysia and Bliss stared at Annis, not saying a word.

"What?" Annis asked.

"You don't call him Lord Brogan," Elysia said.

"When necessary I do," Annis said, annoyed she had not caught her mistake.

"Things are changing here much too rapidly," Bliss said. "I fear I cannot protect you both as I should."

"You cannot protect us forever," Annis cautioned.

"I do not want either of you forced into marriage. I would do anything to prevent that," Bliss said and turned worried eyes on Elysia. "You need to be cautious around Clyde. He has it in his mind to wed you."

"Not likely," Annis said. "He raises his hand far too easily and far too often. No woman is safe with him. Saber, on the other hand…" Annis smiled.

Elysia blushed.

"I must agree with Annis on this. Saber appears a good man. It might be wise to wed him," Bliss said.

Elysia's blush deepened. "He has made no mention of marriage and I barely know him."

"He purposely comes here for you to tend his finger that needs no more tending," Annis said.

"He comes here to drink the brew and take the syrup for his throat," Elysia corrected.

"That is nothing more than an excuse," Annis said. "Anyone can see that he favors you and let me point out that I think you favor him as well."

Elysia's cheeks flamed red.

Annis grinned. "Those glowing cheeks of yours prove my point."

"That is not so," Elysia argued.

"There is nothing wrong in favoring a man," Bliss said. "A marriage is better off if a man and woman at least favor each other. It is a chance for them to fall in love and be happy. And that is something I very much want for you, Elysia, and you as well, Annis."

A sudden shout and loud voice from outside had them jumping. "Chieftain Emory has ordered everyone to gather in front of the keep for an announcement. Do not delay." He repeated it, his words fading as he continued on.

The three women reached out to grab hold of one another's hands. Not one of them said a word, too fearful to voice their thoughts.

The three did as ordered and left the cottage without delay and followed along with other villagers who made their way to the keep. Whispers were shared and worries seen on most faces as the crowd moved forward. Many stared at Annis, and though many thought she was the one chosen to wed Lord Brogan, none dared say anything.

Bliss held tight to her sisters' hands. A plan had been brewing in her mind ever since the possibility of Annis being chosen had proved likely. She did not know if it would work, but she had given it much thought and had even prepared for any objections that might surface. She was ready to see it through if necessary, no matter the consequences.

The three sisters remained in the middle of the crowd, waiting along with everyone else for whatever announcement was to be made.

"It could be something entirely unexpected," Elysia whispered.

"Do not be naïve, Elysia," Annis scolded.

"Not naïve, hopeful," Elysia said.

"You are far too thoughtful and kind," Annis scolded again and smiled. "But I love you anyway."

"And I, you," Elysia assured her, tears tickling at her eyes.

"All will be well," Bliss reassured them as she had done so many times when needed since they had been young.

"Now who is naïve?" Annis asked.

"Hopeful," Elysia repeated again with a smile that showed more worry than confidence.

Chieftain Emory stepped out of the keep, Lawler and Cadell following behind him.

Chieftain Emory was a man of wide girth and moderate height. His long gray hair was secured away from a face that had aged well for more than sixty years. He stood with his shoulders back and his chest wide and he kept his eyes straight ahead, not looking at anyone in particular.

His voice boomed out across the crowd. "A decision has been made concerning a wife for Lord Brogan."

Silence hung heavy, breaths were held, hearts pounded in chests, and fear churned stomachs.

Chieftain Emory kept his voice loud and strong. "I am pleased and proud to announce that Lord Brogan of the Clan MacRae will take a woman from our clan as his wife. The lucky lass is… Annis!"

Chapter Nine

Cheers and shouts of joy rang out. All were relieved that it was finally done, not so Annis or her sisters. Bliss and Elysia huddled protectively around her. The crowd spread apart making room for Cadell as he hurriedly approached Annis.

"You will come with me," Cadell ordered.

Bliss and Elysia stepped forward with her sister.

"Only Annis," Cadell ordered curtly.

"We go with her," Bliss said, her tongue as curt as Cadell's.

Cadell's tongue remained abrupt. "You will say your goodbyes and leave."

Annis wondered if this was what it felt like when being taken to the gallows? Her every step was so heavy she did not think she could take another. She had thought of a hundred ways to avoid this moment and none were even remotely possible. A powerful lord had issued a command and it would be obeyed.

Brogan's words greeted her upon entering the Great Hall. "I will not marry her!"

Annis's heart felt as if it leapt in her chest. Was there a chance this would not happen? Did his refusal to wed her mean anything? The thought sobered Annis to the problem. He did not want her as a wife. What then would their marriage be like if they were both forced on each other?

Her strength returned to her, perhaps a bit too strongly. "I will see him dead before I wed him."

"If only you could end my hell," Brogan retaliated.

"ENOUGH!" Lawler shouted. "This will be done, whether either of you want it or not. You will be joined as husband and wife. How you fare after that is up to you both. Your father, Lord Balloch, signed the necessary documents for you to wed as soon as a woman was found. I need only add your name and the cleric who waits in Lord Emory's solar will conduct a quick ceremony." He turned a sharp glance on Annis. "You need not say a word since everything was already completed by proxy." He looked from Annis to Brogan. "This is done, nothing can change it."

Bliss stepped forward. "May I speak with you alone before this is done?"

"There is nothing you can say that will change this," Lawler warned.

"Just a moment of your time, please," Bliss pleaded.

"Very well," Lawler said annoyed. "But only a moment."

Annis latched onto Bliss's arm. "There is nothing you can do."

"It does not hurt to try. Now watch over each other," Bliss said, looking to each of her sisters. "This will not take long."

Elysia hooked her arm around Annis and they huddled close as they watched Bliss walk off with Chieftain Emory.

"Give us a moment, Cleric William," Lawler said, after entering the solar and holding the door open for the cleric to take his leave. "Make haste, woman, for I will see one lord finally wed," he ordered as soon as he shut the door.

"You are tasked, sir, are you not with finding the cursed lord a wife?" Bliss asked, trying to keep the anxious tremor that ran through her out of her voice.

"I have, but—"

Bliss did not let him finish. "A task that has proven most difficult, has it not?"

"It has but—"

Once again, she did not let him finish. "What if I were to agree to wed the cursed lord in exchange for Annis being freed from marrying Lord Brogan?"

Lawler smiled and shook his head. "That is no bargain at all. I could easily take both of you as wives for the two lords."

"You could, but that would not be a wise choice," Bliss said, her voice having grown more confident.

"Why not?" Lawler asked curiously.

"If you accept my offer, I will wed the cursed lord willingly and being a healer I would do everything I could to heal him. I also would make sure there was at least a chance that I would bear him a bairn, hopefully a son, securing an heir for Lord Lochlann and the Clan MacClaren." Bliss could see that she had stirred interest and that Lawler was giving her proposal thought, and she continued to convince him. "I am a fine healer and I have no doubt that I am the only healer who would make such a generous offer. There is much I may be able to do for Lord Rannick if given the chance. I am sure his father would be pleased to know that you have found his son not only an agreeable wife, but a healer as well."

Lawler rubbed his chin. "And you would do this all willingly without complaint no matter what you faced when meeting Lord Rannick?"

Bliss squared her shoulders and lifted her head a notch. "As long as you spare Annis from marrying Lord Brogan and Elysia as well or Lord Fergus's son, the other cursed lord in need of a wife, I would do it all willingly with no complaint, and on that, you have my word."

Lawler smiled. "You bargain wisely, thinking I would replace Elysia with Annis, something I did give thought to."

"You can find other women to wed the other two cursed lords, but it would continue to prove difficult to find someone to wed Lord Rannick, the one more cursed than the other two."

"I hate to admit it, but you are right," Lawler said. "Let us see how serious you are." He opened the door and summoned the cleric.

***

"What do you think is going on in there?" Annis whispered to Elysia.

"I have no idea, but Bliss has always found a way of protecting us," Elysia said, holding on to hope.

"Not this time," Annis said.

Cadell grinned as if tasting victory. "You are lucky you go to Lord Brogan and not Lord Rannick, the one known as the cursed lord. He is not fit for any woman."

"Watch your tongue, Cadell," Lord Brogan

warned. "Lord Rannick is a longtime friend of mine."

"You would want Annis to wed him instead of you, for that can be arranged," Cadell said, his grin turning to a sneer.

Brogan turned a fierce glare on Cadell that quickly wiped the sneer from his face.

"This curse does not need to be fed. It needs a solution," Elysia said.

"Don't you think solutions have been tried?" Cadell asked as if Elysia understood nothing.

"Endless times and to no avail," Brogan said, turning his head to the flames in the hearth as memories took hold of him.

"Perhaps you were not looking in the right places," Annis suggested.

Brogan's head shot up and he glared at her. "You think you could do better."

Annis nodded. "I do not think. I know I could."

Brogan's scowl darkened. "Then find a way to break the curse after we wed and I will set you free."

"That's not possible," Cadell said, "setting her free, I mean. Your father made careful provisions that the marriage would last or it will be Annis who suffers for it."

Brogan released several oaths and Annis was glad to hear them, for she would have released several herself if she could.

"Be grateful," Cadell chided. "It could be worse for the both of you. At least you favor each other."

"I do not favor her," Brogan snapped sharply.

"And I certainly do not favor him," Annis said with a wince as if it hurt to even think it.

Brogan nodded at Annis. "Besides, she has a weak stomach and will faint far too often with as much blood as I spill."

"Maybe if you stopped acting like a spoiled arse, you would not spill senseless blood," Annis retaliated.

"Annis!" Elysia warned, tugging at her sister's arm.

Cadell grinned and filled a tankard with ale to enjoy while watching the two spar.

"And perhaps if you did not go dictating to men how to build a structure you would still be able to learn something from them," Brogan said, taking a step toward her.

Annis sprang forward. "Learn something from men who are too embarrassed to admit that a woman knew more than the lot of them put together, so they shun her? And I am generous calling them men. They are nothing more than weak fools—much like yourself."

Brogan stepped closer until their bodies almost touched. "A fool maybe, but weak I am not. And this fool will keep his distance from you."

Annis turned a wicked grin on him. "And yet here you stand nearly plastered against me."

Brogan swore beneath his breath and stepped away from her. "You are the most…most…"

"The word you search for is intelligent—something I doubt you are accustomed to in a woman," Annis said and heard her sister Elysia groan.

Cadell laughed and saluted the couple with his tankard before taking a generous gulp.

"Bliss!" Elysia called out when her sister entered the room with Lawler.

Bliss hurried to her sisters. "All is well. You are both safe and free to wed whoever you choose."

"Is this so?" Brogan demanded of Lawler.

"It is," Lawler confirmed.

Cadell sprang to his feet. "This can't be so. It was agreed upon."

"A better deal was struck," Lawler said.

"Better deal?" Annis asked, worry turning her eyes wide as she looked to Bliss. "What did you do?"

"What I had to do," Bliss said, fighting to keep her calm with what was about to come.

Elysia paled. "Good Lord, Bliss, what did you do?"

Lawler smiled. "She married Lord Rannick."

"No! No! No!" Elysia cried. "You cannot wed him."

"Elysia is right. The thought is utter nonsense. I will wed Brogan," Annis said, looking to him and hoping he would agree and help save her sister.

"Annis is right," Brogan said. "Rannick is not fit to wed anyone. Annis and I will wed and be done with it."

"Then it is done. We will wed," Annis said, sending Brogan a grateful look.

Lawler shook his head. "You don't understand. It is done. Bliss is now Lord Rannick's wife. The documents are signed, the seal affixed, and the ceremony complete. And Annis and Elysia are free to wed any man they choose."

Elysia collapsed down on a bench, her legs turning far too weak to hold her.

Annis stared in disbelief at Bliss, at a loss for words.

"Why not wed Annis and Brogan anyway?" Cadell

asked as if what Lawler had agreed to made no sense.

"Bliss does this willingly," Lawler explained.

"What difference does that make?" Cadell asked.

"We could have two wives with only one more to find."

"And find them we will, but Lord Lochlann will be more than pleased with the woman we have secured for Lord Rannick. She is a fine healer who promises to help heal Lord Rannick and promises to do her best to deliver an heir to the Clan MacClaren and do it all willingly and without complaint."

Cadell smiled. "Lord Lochlann will be pleased to hear that."

"You cannot do this, Lawler," Brogan said. "Rannick isn't fit to be a husband to any woman and you know it."

"What I know is that I was tasked with finding a wife for Lord Rannick and I found her, and she is a far better woman than I expected to find. She will do well for Lord Rannick. And as I said, it is done and it cannot be undone," Lawler said and turned a gentle smile on Bliss. "Now gather your things. We leave within the hour."

"No!" Elysia shouted, jumping up from the bench.

Bliss hurried to wrap her arm around her sister. "Come, we do not have much time." She reached her hand out to Annis and she grasped hold of it.

The three left the keep, holding tight to each other as they made their way to their cottage, paying no mind to the stares they received along the way.

Tears fell as Bliss began to gather what few personal items she had. She had lived in fear of losing Annis to Brogan and having to face a moment like this.

A moment when it felt as if her heart shattered completely, the pain of parting so terrible. The only thing that consoled her was that her two sisters would not be forced to wed men who would bring them nothing but pain and suffering.

"You should not have done this," Annis scolded, not fighting the tears that soaked her cheeks.

The pain of her sisters' tears ripped at Bliss like a sharp knife. "There was no other way to keep you both safe."

"We will never see you again," Elysia said, her head drooping with the painful knowledge.

Bliss used the edge of her shawl to wipe away Elysia's tears. "Once I settle in my new home, I will see how things are there. I hope there will be a way for you both to join me, but I don't know if that will be possible or even how long it might take to see it done."

Annis fisted her hands at her sides. "What if there isn't any time?"

"You must be patient," Bliss urged, fighting her churning stomach that warned patience might not be of any help.

"Lord Rannick lost three wives," Annis reminded what failed to be said. "How long do you think you will last wed to him?"

"Good Lord, Bliss, Annis is right," Elysia said, realizing what it truly meant for Bliss to be wed to the cursed lord.

"Do you honestly believe the curse will not touch you?" Annis asked, angry that she had not paid mind to Bliss's endless warnings about Brogan. Bliss should not have to suffer for her foolishness. She should have been the one to wed today.

"I will do my best to see that it doesn't," Bliss said, praying silently for the courage to do so.

"No, what you are doing is sparing Elysia and me from seeing what may happen to you," Annis accused. "At least if I married Brogan my life would not have been in danger."

"We don't know that and I was not willing to take the chance," Bliss said and shook her head when Annis continued to argue. "Please let it be, Annis. Wrong or right, it is done. You both need to find good husbands so you are not left vulnerable again, and hopefully we will all be together again one day." She turned a gentle smile on Elysia. "I believe Saber would make you a good husband. I see the fondness in his eyes when he looks at you and how tender he is with you. Do not let his height and bulk intimidate you. He seems a good man and most importantly, he would keep you safe." With tears brimming in her eyes once again, Bliss turned to Annis. "Mind your tongue the best you can and see that you both keep safe. You know where the coins are. Use them if needed."

"You taught us well. We will survive and we will not stay apart long," Annis said, reaching out to grasp Bliss's hand, wanting to keep hold of her, not let go, but knowing she had no choice.

"It is time," Bliss said. It didn't matter what she faced when she met the cursed lord, nothing could be more painful than saying goodbye to her sisters.

They stood in a tight circle and hugged with strength and love. Tears fell and hearts could almost be heard breaking and the most difficult thing they did was let one another go.

Bliss went to the door, paused a moment before reaching for the latch, since once she stepped outside her life would change forever. She took a fortifying breath and opened the door and stopped, not taking a step, shocked by the amount of villagers lined along the pathway.

Annis took Bliss's healing sack from her and Elysia slipped the other bundle from under Bliss's arm. They kept a short distance behind her as people reached out, thanking her for her sacrifice. Women and daughters cried in sorrow for Bliss and relief for themselves, men bobbed their heads in respect, and prayers were promised for her. Their kindness touched Bliss's heart.

Lawler and Cadell waited outside the keep beside their horses and a third horse waited as well. Brogan was nowhere to be seen.

Chieftain Emory approached Bliss before she reached Lawler and Cadell. "You do a brave thing for the Clan Loudon, Bliss. I am proud of you and I will make sure your sisters are kept safe."

"Thank you, Chieftain Emory," Bliss said, fighting the sorrow of her departure and the fear of what her decision would bring her.

"Come, we must be on our way," Lawler ordered.

Cadell stepped forward and took the bundle from Annis and the one from Elysia and secured them to the horse Bliss would ride.

Bliss hurried to give her sisters one last hug and to assure them that all would be well, then without delay she let Cadell help her mount the horse. She sent a forced smile and a heartfelt wave to her sisters before turning away and following between Lawler and Cadell. She did not glance back for one last look, for fear of bursting into uncontrollable tears. Her sisters were safe and that was all that mattered.

Elysia held tight to Annis, letting her tears flow freely, as they watched Bliss ride away. "I cannot believe this is happening."

Anger held back Annis's tears, though they pooled heavily in her eyes. "I should have known she would do something like this. She has always sacrificed for us."

"This is more than sacrifice. Bliss is giving her life for us." Elysia shook her head. "We cannot let her die. We must do something."

"We are not going to," Annis said and grabbed her sister's hand. "Come on, we have things to do that cannot wait."

Chapter Ten

The silence and no delicious scent of food brewing was a sharp reminder of their sister's absence when Annis and Elysia entered their cottage and both brushed away tears.

Annis tried to shake away the pain of seeing Bliss ride away, but the dreadful image lingered, jabbing repeatedly at her. She knew what she had to do.

"There is only one way to keep the curse from claiming Bliss," Annis said. "The curse has to be broken."

Elysia pressed a firm hand to her churning stomach. "I knew you would think that, but others have tried and failed."

Annis's green eyes shot wide with bold determination. "I have not tried and I refuse to fail. I will find the witch in the hills and finally put an end to this curse."

"You cannot go off on your own. It is too dangerous," Elysia warned. "Please, Annis, do not be foolish."

"There is no one to go with me," Annis argued.

Elysia tapped her chest. "I will go with you."

"You cannot." Annis shut her eyes briefly against a sudden image that struck her, the possible consequences of Bliss's decision. "If Bliss needs tending, she will reach out to you. You need to stay here."

Elysia cringed. "I cannot bear the thought of her suffering for us."

"I agree, which is why I need to do this."

Elysia had a sudden thought. "Lord Brogan! He wants the curse ended. He would go with you."

"He tried finding the witch in the hills and failed."

"More the better," Elysia said. "He can make sure you do not waste time looking where he has already searched."

Annis did not want to admit her sister was right and she certainly did not want to ask Brogan to join her in her quest, not that he'd probably agree, but if Bliss could sacrifice, so could she.

"Go now and find Lord Brogan before he takes his leave," Elysia urged, shoving Annis toward the door.

Annis opened the door to find Clyde ready to enter. "What are you doing here. There is no healer to tend anyone anymore."

"Elysia will do as a healer for now and she will need a husband to keep her safe especially from the likes of you," Clyde said and went to step forward.

Annis raised a fist to him and snarled a warning. "Take one more step and I'll break your nose."

Clyde stepped back quickly. "I am going to Chieftain Emory and request to wed Elysia, and since he promised to keep you both safe, I am sure he will be pleased to accept my offer. Once Elysia and I are wed, I will deal with you, Annis."

"We are free to choose our own husbands and you are not even on that list. Now go!" Annis shouted and Clyde walked away grumbling. She turned to Elysia. "Come with me while I talk with Lord Brogan."

"How is it that Clyde backs away when you threaten him?" Elysia asked, hurrying along with her sister.

"He knows I will do what I threaten and he will not take the chance of suffering the shame of getting his nose broken by a woman."

Elysia had to smile at the image her sister's remark provoked.

Annis left Elysia's side in a rush when they reached the keep and she saw Brogan getting ready to mount his horse. "I need you," she shouted and almost bit her tongue when she realized how it sounded.

Brogan smiled and spread his arms wide. "I'm all yours, *mo ghràdh*."

Annis stopped in front of him and planted her hands on her hips. "I am not and never will be your love."

"Remember what I warned you about saying never," he teased with a wink and rested his arms across his chest. "So tell me what you need from me."

His commanding stance made it seem he was ready to battle with her while his handsome features easily distracted. She was grateful neither intimidated her, but she had to mind her tongue if she wanted his help. She also had to remember that he was a nobleman and she a peasant.

"I need your help in rescuing my sister," Annis said.

Brogan's smile faded. "I wish I could help you, but after speaking with Lawler there is nothing that can be done. She is wed to Rannick and nothing will change that."

"I know nothing will change that. What I want to prevent is my sister's imminent death. The curse will surely claim her and I will not sit idle and wait for that to happen. I must break the curse."

"Please help us," Elysia pleaded softly. "Or Annis will go off alone in search of the witch in the hills and I worry she will never return."

"You will do no such thing," Brogan warned with a snip of anger. "I have told you that I have searched endlessly for a way to end the curse to no avail. And you will only waste time in chasing the myth of the witch in the hills."

His reminder of what he once told her, reminded her of something else he had said. "What did you mean when you told me the curse could not be broken that it had to be fulfilled, but it was impossible to do?"

Brogan shook his head at Annis. "You are not going to give up, are you?"

She mimicked him, crossing her arms over her chest to show her determination and her chin went up a notch. "No. I am going to save my sister no matter what it takes and I intend to do it with or without your help."

Brogan kept his arms crossed over his chest, afraid he'd reach out and try to shake some sense into her. "Then let me explain to you, as it was explained to me by endless wise women, why your quest will fail. The strongest of curses is the one cast by a dying person. Lady Aila of the Clan MacWilliam cursed three clan leaders before she died, my father, Lord Balloch of the Clan MacRae, Lord Fergus of the Clan MacBridan, and Rannick's father, Lord Lochlann of Clan MacClaren. Lord Lochlann was cursed to suffer the most since he had been good friends to Lord Brochan, Lady Aila's husband. The task of the three men was to see that the Clan MacWilliam bloodline never continued. They battled with the Clan MacWilliam to wipe it out, make sure not a single MacWilliam lived. There was only one left to be killed, Wynda, the two-day-old daughter of Lady Aila and Lord Brochan."

Elysia gasped. "To kill an innocent bairn is reprehensible."

"I agree," Brogan said. "Wisely, Lady Aila managed to get her daughter to safety. Unfortunately, not for long. The daughter was found and killed. To break the curse, the wrong that had been done to the Clan MacWilliam, had to be made right and that could only have been done through the only living MacWilliam heir—the daughter. So you see, the curse will continue through generations unless Rannick, Odran, and myself produce no heirs and let the curse die along with our bloodlines. Otherwise any heir to be born to any of us is doomed to a life of eternal hell."

"How do you know the daughter was killed?" Annis asked, having always been skeptical of tales by boasting men and those who accomplished the feat of wiping out the Clan MacWilliam surely would have made sure it was known they succeeded where others had failed.

"My father was there to witness it," Brogan said.

Annis had more questions for him. "How did your father know it was the MacWilliam daughter? And how could he be sure it was the right bairn? Did she have any specific marks on her that could attest to her identity?"

"From what my father said, they tracked down the faithful servant, Gunna, that Lady Aila had entrusted her daughter with and she confirmed it was the MacWilliam bairn."

"So in the end, this faithful servant betrayed Lady Aila?" Annis asked.

"She was left no choice. It was her or the bairn's life."

Annis still wasn't finished. "How many people witnessed this?"

"My father and Lord Lochlann. They believed by seeing the infant lass dead that the curse would be no more or at least lose some of its power." Brogan shook his head. "They were wrong."

"What if the faithful servant lied?" Annis asked.

"Her life was at stake and enough questions. This is done and you will go on no foolish quest," Brogan ordered, having hoped to discourage her with the truth, but he could see from the determined look on Annis's face that she had no intention of obeying him. "You may be stubborn, Annis, but you are no fool. Think of the risk… alone and vulnerable, no horse to carry you, the unpredictable weather to battle and in the end no way to see the curse broken."

"Is that what you truly believe or are you afraid I will do what you could not? Succeed!"

Brogan's eyes narrowed as he stepped closer to Annis. "You will not do this, Annis. I will make sure of it."

Her chin went up high. "Hasn't your clan and the two other clans brought enough suffering and pain to people."

Elysia tugged at her sister's arm. "We should go. Lord Brogan is right. It is too dangerous a journey for you to make alone."

"At least one sister is wise enough to do the right thing," Brogan said.

Elysia squeezed Annis's arm. "I will see my sister kept safe."

Brogan laughed, though there was no smile on his face. "I fear that is an impossible task."

"Safe journey, sir," Elysia said and tugged her sister along, away from Lord Brogan.

"You kn—"

"Not a word till we get home," Elysia cautioned as they walked away.

Annis held her tongue, though it was difficult.

"There was no point in arguing with Lord Brogan and I wouldn't be surprised if he was speaking with Chieftain Emory right now, warning him about your intentions. So if you insist on doing this, you better leave before someone tries to stop you," Elysia said once inside the cottage.

Annis hugged her sister. "I am going to find the witch in the hills, but not to break the curse."

Elysia shook her head as she gathered food to wrap in a cloth for Annis. "I don't understand, if not for that, then why seek her out?"

Annis got busy gathering what she would need. "I do not believe the MacWilliam bairn died, and that is what I seek from the witch. I want to know if the infant bairn died all those years ago or if she still lives? If she does, I intend to ask the witch how the wrong can be made right, then I am going to find the woman and see this curse ended. I do not think the faithful servant who Lady Aila trusted with her daughter's life would betray her. She no doubt gave her word to Lady Aila to keep the bairn from harm."

"Then what bairn was sacrificed," Elysia asked.

Annis shook her head. "No bairn was sacrificed."

"Are you suggesting they never found the bairn?"

"It was a lie to save themselves from failure."

Annis took hold of her sister's hand. "I do not know how long this will take me. A week, a month, or more, and I fear leaving you alone, especially with Clyde sniffing around you. Bliss was right. Saber is a good man and will see you kept safe. It is obvious that you favor him and that he favors you. You need to marry him right away or else I fear what Clyde might do to force you to wed him."

"I do not have the courage to ask Saber to wed me?" Elysia confessed.

"You think Bliss had the courage to do what she did or I have the courage to do what I am about to do? We do it for one another, to make sure we all stay safe. Bliss would not worry over you if she knew you wed Saber and I would not worry over you if I know you will find your courage and wed Saber. Besides, one of us deserves to be happy and I see how happy you and Saber are when you are together."

"What if he says no?" Elysia asked.

"I do not believe he will, but you need to be prepared for such a possibility," Annis said, rubbing her brow in thought.

Both sisters jumped at the knock at the door.

Annis went and opened it cautiously. "Lendra."

"I haven't much time and either have you, Annis," Lendra said, forcing Annis to step back as she entered and shut the door. "Your mum was a good friend, so I have come to warn you. Lord Brogan has ordered Chieftain Emory to make sure that neither of you leave the village until further notice." She turned worried eyes on Annis. "He gathers two warriors now to keep watch over you. Whatever you intend to do, Annis, don't delay and may God be with you and your sisters."

"You must go now," Elysia said as soon as Lendra left and hurried to gather the few coins Bliss had managed to save in case they were ever needed. "Take these, you may need them.

Annis took the small pouch and opened it to share some of the coins with Elysia. "You may need some as well."

"No, I need none," Elysia insisted. "You will need them more than me. Remember Bliss told us about how the witch of the hills demands a price for her magic. I only hope the coins will suffice."

"Whatever the price, I will pay it. I can do no less since Bliss pays a higher price to keep us safe." Annis reached out and hugged her sister tight, then held her at arms' length. "You need to do the same, though your price will not be nearly as dear. I need to know you will always be protected."

Elysia eased her sister's worry. "I will gather my courage and seek a marriage with Saber. You have my word. Now go before I stop you from going."

Annis slipped on her cloak, pulling the hood over her head and with her small bundle in hand, she left the cottage and disappeared into the woods.

Elysia stood by the hearth, tears running down her cheeks. How in just a few short hours had life changed so drastically? Losing one sister today had been unbearable, losing two broke her heart completely.

The creak of the door opening had Elysia turning with fright only to sigh in relief when she saw Lendra.

"I did not want to tell you in front of your sister, for fear of what she would do, but you need to know," Lendra said. "Bliss was barely gone when Chieftain Emory talked about seeing you and Annis wed."

Elysia paled. "That can't be. Bliss secured our freedom to choose our own husbands."

"Chieftain Emory is a sly man. He will find a way to have it his way and to also make certain he need no longer concern himself about you or Annis, thus keeping his word to your sister about seeing you and Annis kept safe."

"Thank you for the warning," Elysia said

Lendra opened the door to leave. "Tongues wag about you and Saber. He would make a good husband. Do whatever you have to do not to wed Clyde. He is a mean one."

Elysia stared at the closed door. Her sisters were brave and did what was needed. Could she be as brave? The silence grew heavier around her and she glanced around the cottage that had always been filled with talk, laughter, and love. She was alone, truly alone. She had never been alone in her life and the thought frightened her beyond words as did what might happen if Clyde should get his way. Fear had her reaching for her cloak and she slipped it on as she hurried out of the cottage and took off running to Saber' croft.

THE END... not really! It's just the beginning of Highland Intrigue Trilogy.

The Silent Highlander
The Condemned Highlander
Highlander the Cursed Lord

Go to www.donnafletcher.com
to find out more!

Printed in Great Britain
by Amazon